Grandma Ida

HELEN KLINE

outskirtspress
DENVER, COLORADO

Grandma Ida

v1.0

Outskirts Press, Inc.
http://www.outskirtspress.com

ISBN: 978-1-4787-4911-0

PRINTED IN THE UNITED STATES OF AMERICA

Grandma Ida sat looking at all the headstones in the Dawson City Memorial Cemetery; she smiled and said, "Did you ever think about all the people that are buried here? For every marker there is a story, and for every story there is a history. I can tell you the story of everyone that is here, I lived it from the very first one, my little sister to the last one my son, Charlie.

"You would think after all the funerals I have attended I would get used to it, but I miss each and every one of them as if it was yesterday. I have outlived them all; I wonder sometimes if there will be anyone left to come to my funeral."

GRANDMA IDA

Grandma Dawson was 100 years old that year and the town of Dawson City, Colorado decided to have a citywide birthday party for her. She had lived at the Senior Nursing home for the last six years. The story is told of how this feisty little old woman, her husband, Charles Dawson along with her sisters, Laura and Maude were threatened, if they did not leave the valley they would be forcibly evicted from their ranch so a reservoir could be built. They put up quite a fight, and in the end they won.

Ida and her sisters were born on this homestead. Her mother, Ingabar, father, John had four boys and five girls; they worked a cattle ranch, had a dude ranch and ran an outfitters hunting camp. Ida was the oldest of the girls that was born on the ranch, two girls died in infancy. Her two older brothers taught Ida the basics of ranching and hard work.

She outlived her entire family, only married once and had five children of her own. One baby was lost at childbirth, and when the measles epidemic swept through the valley, most of the small children in the area died, including two of her own babies. They were buried in the family cemetery, beside Grandma and Grandpa Lawson.

Her story was in all the newspapers in Colorado. Shannon worked for the *Denver Post* at the time. When the editor called her into his office, he told her she was to go to Dawson City and get the story on some old woman by the name of Ida Ingabar Dawson.

Shannon snickered, "You got to be kidding; I am a city girl now and wouldn't know how to act in some little old hick town, much less go see an old woman in a nursing home. Don't those places smell like old dying people?"

He gave her a stern look and said, "Careful what you say, you might end up in one of those places someday." Then he laughed and said, "You will be leaving tomorrow. Here is the map, knock yourself out." With that he walked out the door, again laughing, then he turned around and said, "Why am I leaving, this is my office? Goodbye, Shannon have a good time." And he walked behind his desk and sat down in his oversized desk chair, crossed his arms, smiled and had the gall to wave his two index fingers at her.

By 8:00 o'clock next morning she was in the rented car heading for Dawson City, located on the Grand Mesa, the closest place to nowhere she could think of. It was a long way and she spent half the day behind the wheel.

By the time she had driven over some of the most spectacular panoramas she had ever seen and steep mountain passes, driving on the twistiest, curvy road she could imagine, she was exhausted and hoping to find a small out of the way motel.

She was beginning to think no one ever stopped in these mountains. Finally, she saw the lights up ahead and a sign that said Dawson City Motel and Dottie's Restaurant. Yes, that sounds good, all she had eaten was some munchies and they had left a nauseous feeling in her stomach. After she parked her rented car in front of the door reading Office, she decided to look this motel over before she went in. It was a one-story building. There were eight rooms with a wooden walkway in front; and an overhead porch roof that hung over the walk below. The motel itself was built of old logs, with chinking between each log. She also observed that hers was the only car in the parking lot, but she thought, "*This isn't the Waldorf, what did you expect",* so she walked to the office and observed a sign on the door, "Register at the restaurant, after you pick out a vacant room, settle in, then come to the restaurant and ask for Dottie." So she chose a room at the far end of the walkway, figuring she wouldn't be disturbed by other people coming and going.

Her room was small but eloquently furnished. The bed was pushed up against one wall, draped in a handmade quilt of blue and white squares, with two white lace pillows leaning against the headboard. The small bed stand next the bed was unvarnished oak, and a small round oak table with one wooden chair of the same unvarnished oak was nestled in the corner. At the opposite wall stood a matching unvarnished oak four-drawer dresser that matched the bed and the nightstand. Shannon could see they had that all the furniture had been hand made. The bathroom had just a shower and a toilet in the corner. Beside it was a porcelain sink stand, with an oval mirror above it. There were two side-by-side white bath towels with a hand towel and a washcloth all with crochet lace on the edges, folded neatly and hung on a small towel holder made of wood next to them.

The bathroom floor tiles were blue and white squares, and the floor in the bedroom was of highly polished pine, with an oval braided rug of many different colors, also looking handmade. On wall behind the table hung a large picture of a beautiful green valley with a river running through it. In the distance, you could see a herd of brown white-faced cattle grazing. On the hill off to the right sat a small house overlooking the river, a bunkhouse behind it, that looked much like the Dawson City Motel and a barn with a fenced in corral where horses were saddled and ready to ride, waiting just behind the bunkhouse.

She gazed at the picture for a long time thinking this was a very good artist's interpretation of paradise, with the surrounding high snow covered mountains rising majestically in the background; it would be the perfect ranch to come home to. She set her suitcase down and thought; "*Okay, now I had better go see this Dottie, how do I lock the door?"However, who is here but you; no one is going to steal anything.* By now, her stomach was telling her to go see if the food was any good at the "Greasy Spoon" Dottie's Restaurant, and ask for Dottie.

From the moment, she walked into the restaurant the waitress greeted her with a smile and a "Hello" and asked, "Are you just checking in or did she want to have supper?" Shannon told her, "Both I guess."

Then Dottie told her she could sit anywhere she wanted and she would be with her in just a moment. She was waiting on a table in the corner where an older couple had been sitting. Shannon couldn't help but overhear them say something about Grandma Ida, and how they were so excited to see her again. The waitress laughed and said, "Everyone is, but she put up quite a fuss about all this fah-de-rah about a birthday."

They said that was expected from her, she did not like too much fussing about. They laughed and then the old man said, "God gave us this old girl as an example to live our lives by, and she set a fine example for many of us."They all nodded in agreement.

The waitress then turned her attention to Shannon, and said, "And what may I get for you, Missy?" "I don't know," Shannon replied. "What is the special?" The old man in the corner yelled over to her and said, "Try the roast beef dinner, No one makes it like Dottie. Besides it's the only thing on the menu for today." He smiled and said, "It also includes a fresh baked blueberry pie with a scoop of homemade ice cream on top." Shannon said, "That sounds good, she was pretty hungry." Dottie just smiled and said, "You had better be." as she walked away, she asked over her shoulder, "Cup of coffee to start you out? "Yes, that would be nice."

"Where you from, Missy?" At first, Shannon was surprised that anyone would be so bold as to ask about her business. However, after a while and a lot of conversation, while she ate her overflowing plate of the delicious dinner, she relaxed and got into the Journalist mode, and started asking questions about the upcoming celebration for Ida Dawson. They were more than anxious to talk about her and her husband, Charles. They told her about Ida's mother and father, John and Ingabar Lawson who came and Homesteaded the Dawson Valley about 1865.

The waitress was beginning to get very busy as more people came into the restaurant. She was taking in guests for the motel and serving dinners at the same time, she had a cook in the kitchen that was about as round as she was tall, but together they made a great team.

They kept up with everyone, no one had to wait very long for their dinner, and some even sat outside on the front porch and waited for their dinner. Dottie would hand it to them and they would sit on the step and eat. Shannon had never seen anything like this and couldn't believe how informal this all was. Everyone knew each other and they would all be talking about their cattle, and the new calves, their ranches or the kids. Shannon just listened and was beginning to enjoy all this comfortable friendly talk. She could hardly wait to get back to her room so she could write about all this.

She suddenly realized that she was so tired and so full from that last piece of pie that by the time she got back to her room she didn't have the energy to do any writing that night. She told herself she would write tomorrow, so she just took a shower and then went straight to bed.

There must have been some kind of magic in that motel, because for the first time in a long time she slept like a baby and did not wake until she heard the sound of a dinner bell in the distance. "What the heck was that?" With a start, she jumped out of bed. Then she heard it again. *I have to find out what that is all about,* she told herself. Within twenty minutes she was dressed and heading down the wooden walk to the restaurant. Then she noticed the dinner bell hanging from an iron rod stuck on the wall of the restaurant. It had a triangle bent bar with a long iron rod tied next to it. When she opened the door, she was greeted with smiles and hellos from around the room, full of people eating plates piled high with pancakes, sausages, and hash brown potatoes. She looked around, found one empty stool, and quickly sat down. Immediately, Dottie had a steaming hot cup of coffee in front of her, and said, "We only have pancakes and sausage for breakfast this morning, tomorrow it will be ham and eggs, will that suit you, Honey?" "Perfect," was Shannon's reply.

When she asked about the dinner bell, she had heard someone said, "That's Dottie's way of letting everyone know breakfast is ready." The old farmer sitting next to Shannon smiled and leaned over to her saying, "Dottie keeps things simple this way, we can either eat what is in front of us or we can stay home and fix what ever we want. Most of us like it this way; we don't have to make any hard decisions." They both laughed at that.

He said his name was Lenny Olson, and he lived just down the road a ways. Shannon laughed to herself and wondered, "*How far is "a ways?"* Oh well, she was beginning to really like these people, thinking, *I could like living here.* Then she remembered she had a job to do. *Come on you have to get back to reality, Dummy, you are a city girl, remember?*

She told Lenny, "My name is Shannon and I am a journalist from the *Denver Post*. I came to interview Grandma Ida and to see what all the fuss was about." He was quiet for a moment then he said, "I know you didn't know Grandma, so I will forgive you, but we don't feel like this is just a lot of, 'Fuss' as you call it. Grandma Ida was and still is everyone's grandmother; she and Charles were the reason we all stayed here for all these years. They would never give up when things were bad, and there was always a place for us to come to when things were bad.

"They made up their bunk house so it would house two and even three families when the Depression hit us all and many of us lost our ranches and were homeless. They would go out and butcher a beef to feed the neighbors. Many of us would get together and hunt down an elk or two and divide it up among all the families, while the others would be lookouts for the game warden and distract or tell him we saw someone in the other county shooting game out of season.

"Grandma and Grandpa Dawson would let us hide it in their barn and butcher it there out of sight. In the winter, we would all gather at their house, and they would set up a communal kitchen. The bunkhouse with private rooms was made up for everyone to sleep, as we waited for spring to come. I don't know how they managed to feed all of us, but later we learned they butchered about twenty of their cattle and Grandma made sure everyone was fed. Every summer they would put in a huge garden and store all the vegetables in a root cellar in the back of their house. I'm sure everyone in this room could tell you stories about them and how they helped them, in their time of crisis, too.

"When the measles epidemic came to this valley, it was Charles and a couple of the other ranchers who traveled over the mountain to get a vaccine insisting the doctor came back with them. The story goes they actually kidnapped him and brought him back, but that of course could be a story, but knowing them, I would be more inclined to believe it. Grandpa and Grandma Dawson lost two of their daughters due to the measles that summer. All those children were buried in their family cemetery, as we are all family here. There is so much more to tell about them, but 'Fuss,' no it is no fuss to us. We loved them. They were mother, father, grandpa, and grandma. To some they were the only family they had."

Many of the people in the restaurant had stopped their talk

and had been listening to Lenny, adding many more stories they remembered as well.

The atmosphere in the restaurant became like a family reunion, with each person telling another story. They laughed at some and there were tears from others. Shannon was wishing she had a tape recorder, or that she could have remembered all that was said that morning or could write it all down as fast as they were telling it. They seemed to need to tell their stories and to remember. There were people standing along the walls listening and nodding their heads remembering their story, but alas the morning rush was past and it was time for lunch. For sure, this moment of time would not pass this way again, and no one wanted to leave. Even Dottie would stop from her duties and listen, the cooking and serving had stopped for a while as everyone listened to the old timers tell of the different things that went on at the Dawson Ranch when it was still the Dawson Ranch over the years .

Shannon did not hear it right away, and then when she heard it again she leaned in to listen, "When it was still the Dawson Ranch." Once again her journalist senses kicked in. "What do you mean when it was still the Dawson Ranch?" she asked. The room became silent for a moment and then someone in the back said, "It is no longer called the Dawson Ranch, it is called Dawson City."

No one answered her question, they all just seemed to stand up and ask Dottie for their bill and they left the restaurant. She looked at Dottie and asked, "What did I say that was wrong? I feel like I just shot the President." Dottie said, "You didn't say anything wrong, Honey. It is just that everyone here had to fight very hard to keep the Dawson Ranch from being buried under water and the Dawson Ranch from becoming the Dawson Reservoir. It would have been a burial ground to most of the old timers around here. As you could hear, they would have had many memories buried under many gallons of water." It is still a fear they all live with and they well remembered those four years of the BLM and the WCA and their bullying tactics.

"How far am I from Dawson City?" Shannon asked. "Just a ways and around the corner." Dottie said, "Go straight on the road a little further, and you can't miss it," she said. "I think I will be staying here for the next couple of weeks," Shannon said and paid for her breakfast using the company credit card for the next two weeks, and then she headed for Dawson City. She was anxious to meet Grandma Dawson.

Dawson City was a small town with only one main street, which ran through the middle of it. She noticed the big building on her left as she left the restaurant. A sign in the yard with an arrow pointing to the left read, "Maude Lawson Charter School, and Museum." Under it, was written, Kindergarten to 8th grade. There was a playground on the side with a slide, a teeter totter, and a court for basketball.

Behind the school, she also noticed a small corral, with six ponies eating hay. Six bridles hung over the fence post, where three small saddles straddled the fence railing. Next to, half full a water trough of water. It looked like something out of the Old West.

Next to the school was a red brick building with big bay doors; above the doors was a sign reading, "Dawson City Volunteer Fire Department." Through the window, she could see two big red fire trucks. The lawn was perfectly groomed, an antique pump wagon sitting there all polished and bright red.

As Shannon continued down the street another antique appeared, a small gas station with two of the old, single red gas pumps that only had regular gas. A sign against the wall of the station said, "Diesel in the Back." It was a self service station with another sign hanging next to the door, painted in neat but bold letters: "If no one's here just leave the money on the counter. Or if it's an IOU put your name and the amount on the tablet next to the cash register and I'll catch up with you and settle up later." Shannon had to laugh at that, as she thought, "*You sure wouldn't do that in Denver, but then again there is only one way out and one way in to Dawson City.*

Another sign reading, "CREDIT CARD, WHATS THAT?" Below that in small letters was written; "Cash only, and if I know you, I will accept a personal check." Shannon knew she was in trouble if there was no bank in town. She drove on a little further and noticed a small grocery store with an attached hardware store next to it on one side of the narrow dirt street.

A tavern about fifty feet further down the street, with a hitching rail set up next to the side of it looked like it had been used many times, as evidenced by the horse droppings near it. Every little town should have one of those. Even at this time of day, one good-looking Quarter horse was tied there, with a bundle of hay for him to munch in the feed box built in front of the railing. Hank Williams music was blaring from inside.

On the other side of the street, she sighed with relief when she saw a sign saying, City Bank of Dawson. The red brick walls seemed out of place, in this town of all board buildings with Cedar Slate Shingle Roofs. Next to, it was a pharmacy with the sign saying, Soda Fountain, Ice Cream Parlor, and post office. Payphone available in back.

There were little shops along the street selling clothing. A gift shop with greeting cards and knick-knacks for the tourists; attached to it was the bait shop complete with fishing gear, rods and paraphernalia. At the end of the street a sign saying "10 miles to Dawson Reservoir." With an arrow painted at the bottom pointing towards a winding dirt road to the east with many gunshot holes in it. Below was a sign that read Peaceful Paradise Nursing Home and Dawson Memorial Cemetery. It showed an arrow pointing to the left, so she turned her car onto the road to go to the nursing home, but changed her mind at the last minute and decided to drive past, just to explore further down the road. She was anxious to see what the cemetery looked like. There was an arched sign that said 'Dawson City Memorial Cemetery, and underneath there was a smaller sign that read, "All who enter please leave all your noise outside." Another sign in bold lettering said. "For every grave marker you see there is a story of the history of Dawson City, Stop and listen." It was fenced in with high woven wire with a latched gate in the center.

Stopping the car, she got out and walked to the gate, lifting the latch to walk among the headstones. There were a couple of large granite headstones, but most were handmade wooden crosses, with names and dates carved into them. One small one with a white picket fence around it had a small baby cradle that was placed in the center of this fenced in gravesite, an inscription carved into the panel that was nailed across the little white gate saying; "Jesus cradles my darling baby now." Ellie Sue Lawson born 1872 died 1873.

Why Shannon stayed there in the cemetery for such a long time she couldn't say? However, for some reason she felt at peace there and the quiet seemed to speak to her; she didn't want to leave. Then as she turned at the end of one of the rows she saw the cross with the large letters spread across two graves that read, "They loved together in life and now they are together for eternity." Below it said, "John and Ingabar Lawson 1913 and 1914." There was no mistaking who they were. Fresh flowers had been placed on the grave, carefully arranged so they spread all the way across both names. Shannon looked away and that was when she saw a large white marble headstone. She walked closer and read the inscription. It said, "Johnny Dandridge," Medal of Honor, died serving his country beyond the call of duty. WWII, 1943. DOB unknown.

It was late afternoon by the time Shannon finally left the cemetery. She decided to go back to Dottie's Restaurant for the rest of the day. She would go to the nursing home tomorrow and ask if she could talk to Ida. She knew she would spend as much time with her as she could, but she figured she would have to ration her time, after all Grandma Ida is a hundred years old. Shannon figured Grandma would be a bit senile and she would have to figure out what was fact and what was not. It was hard for Shannon to visualize what a hundred year old woman looked like; she had never seen or even visited with one before. She must be pretty wrinkled and bent over, with thin hair and gnarly fingers, and eyes that were dull with age.

Since the evening dinner rush had not yet began Shannon, decided to ask Dottie what Ida was like and would she have to take her time and speak very slow so she could understand her? Dottie looked at her and then she laughed, "Sweetie, I would give a hundred dollars to be there when you meet Grandma Ida," but she did not say a word about what that meant or what to expect. Dottie just turned, laughing went back to help in the kitchen to get ready for the evening rush.

Next morning Shannon went in to the restaurant for breakfast, and everyone turned to look at her. One man said, "I hear you are going to see that old senile woman in the nursing home today." She looked at Dottie, she just shrugged and said, "You know how small town folks are, everyone knows everyone's business," as she laughed and went to get Shannon's cup of coffee accompanied with her ham and eggs.

After breakfast, her first stop would have to be the telephone to call her boss to let him know she needed cash. He laughed when she told him about the night before and all the stories about Ida and Charlie.

He seemed pleased she had made contacts, and then he gave her an expense account number for the bank, saying have fun and then he hung up. Shannon was at the bank when it opened at nine o'clock. She was sent to the office of the President of the bank. He was a tall lean man about thirty five and "Just God Awful Handsome."

He was wearing a Western type shirt under a nice Western tweed jacket, with the leather yolk in the back and on the front shoulders. She couldn't help but notice the Stetson hat hanging on the coat rack in his office. Her first thought was, "*Oh boy, I have to explain my situation to another cowboy.*"

As he reached, his hand out to her and said, "Hello, my name is Charles Dawson, what I can do for you?" Shannon felt she must have looked pretty stupid when she opened her mouth to speak and nothing came out.

He waited for a second, just enough time for her to come to her senses. She reached out her hand and said, "My name is Shannon Campbell, I am a journalist from Denver, and I work for the Denver Post. I have come to see Mrs. Ida Dawson, but I realize all the businesses here take cash, so I need to open an account with you, assigned to me from my headquarters in Denver." He was still holding her hand, or was she still holding his? He looked at their hands, then at her, and then he said, "Perhaps we should sit down and I will need some information."

With that, he motioned for her to sit in the chair on the other side of his desk. As she let go of his hand and sat down, she thought, "H*e must think I am some kind of doofus*." She finally regained her senses and said, "I must apologize, I didn't expect to be talking to a Charles Dawson."

He smiled and said, "I am named after my grandfather and my father that makes me Charles Dawson the third. The first was Called Charles, Number 2 was Charlie and they called me Chucky. I always hated that, so after my dad and grandpa passed I changed my name. I figure there were too many juniors to explain, and now that they are all gone, I just refer to myself as Charles." "Do you have a son you call Charlie?" she asked before she realized what a stupid question that was. It was also none of her business. He laughed and said, "I'm not married and I think not. Now shall we figure out how to get you some money?"

It took about a half hour and all was set up with the Denver Post for her to have an expense account. She really felt, she needed to go and see Grandma Ida. Charles told her, "I think you will like her, but she is a crafty old girl, she doesn't like to talk about herself, she will turn the questions around and you will answer more then she will." Shannon figured she was a good journalist and could handle this "little old lady." How little Shannon knew.

From the moment, she walked into the nursing facility all her impressions of a nursing home changed. She had ever been in this brightest, most simply furnished, freshest smelling building. It did not have that hospital sterile smell about it. Actually she could smell the slight scent of lilacs.

As she walked through the door, to her right was the registry desk. To her left she noticed a dining room with a large dormer of windows overlooking a beautiful garden with flowers lining a walkway and a huge lilac tree, with double petal blossoms shading part of the gazebo in the center of the court. There were people sitting on the benches chatting and laughing, some were just sitting listening. Shannon thought, "*I'm sure this is as old as Dawson City.*" Straight ahead of her was a wall making a turn to the right to the rooms beyond, down a long corridor with windows on the west side of the building.

She immediately went to the registers counter and explained who she was and what her purpose was. The lady behind the counter smiled and said,"Just give me a moment and I will be right back." After she left Shannon looked around and noticed the same picture hanging in the waiting room that was in her hotel room, but this one was an original oil painting, and signed Charles Dawson 1906.

The nurse came back with an orderly who said, "Grandma Ida is as ready as she will ever be, follow me."Then she turned and looked at the nurse at the counter and laughed just a slight quiet laugh. They both were smiling. Shannon thought, "*What is so funny? Everyone does that all the time when I ask about Ida."*

As they walked down the hall a couple of old ladies sitting in chairs wriggled their feet in a tub of water, Looking like they were half asleep, but just as Shannon and the orderly got in front of them, the orderly stepped aside and pointed her finger at them. About that time, Shannon was right in front of them and they woke up, started to kick their feet, and splashed water all over her. They were giggling and clapping their hands, nudging each other, they were having a great time getting her all wet.

She just stood there and looked at them both; one was a bit on the heavy side and had rosy cheeks that looked like she might have been Mrs. Santa Claus. The other was a small spry little lady with a head of white curly hair that went every which way.

Shannon made a quick survey of her and would guess her to be about five feet tall, weighing about ninety pounds. She could just barely touch the floor when she put her feet down. She had perfect white teeth and she was smiling. Then she spoke in a very clear sweet voice, "I understand you want to talk to me about some newspaper thing?"

"Are you Ida Ingabar Dawson?" Shannon asked surprised. "My God," she said. "Nobody has called me by my given name in years, how did you know that?" "I am a journalist," she said, "I have to be sure of everything, and get all the facts right."

The two old ladies looked at each other made a face. The orderly looked at Ida and said, "Now, Grandma, you be nice to this lady, she has come from a long way to see and talk to you." Shannon learned later that the orderly was Ida's great granddaughter, Lorraine. She would need Lorraine a lot in the next few weeks, and they became very good friends.

"Where are you from?" Grandma Ida asked. So explaining why she was here Shannon told her, "I came from Denver." "No, no, where are *you* from?" she persisted. 'Don't you have a home where you came from? Nobody would come' from Denver."

"Oh," she said, "you mean where I was raised? I was born and raised in a small town in the northern woods of Minnesota. I lived there until I was seventeen, where I graduated from high school and then went to college, after which I got a job working for a small newspaper in Minneapolis. Until I was hired to do field work for the Denver Post, where I eventually moved."

Shannon did not know why she was telling so much about herself. Ida just looked at her then she said, "I didn't need your whole life's history." But since I got it, I may as well ask, are you married?" "No." "Good, you probably would talk too much for a man anyway," she said. Then the two old women laughed.

Shannon was becoming irritated as she thought, "*Why, you mean, cantankerous old woman, you tricked me. Charles told me to be careful, didn't he? Okay if that's how it's going to be, I'll play your game, but you don't know how stubborn I can be.*"

She asked her a few more unimportant questions just to see how she would react to questions, and she answered them. It was becoming obvious that Grandma Ida was tiring of Shannon, so she asked her, "Would it be alright if I came back after lunch?" She said she takes a nap for about an hour after lunch. Shannon asked then what would be a good time for her, and she said about two o'clock. Shannon needed that time to regroup and maybe find a better way to approach her interview.

As she closed the door to the Peaceful Paradise Nursing home, Lorraine followed her out. She said, "Don't let Grandma get to you, she will needle you till you give up and leave. She has done it to other people, who have tried to interview her, but she has quite a story to tell and it needs to be told, I think you can do it. I will try to help the best way that I can." Then she said, "I'm going home I have had a long shift and I'm tired."

"By the way call me, Lorrie, everyone else does." I'm Shannon." "I know." "Oh yeah, I remembered this is a small town and everyone knows everyone business. No secrets here."

Lorrie just laughed and walked away, saying almost under her breath, "Yeah."

For the next few days, Shannon traveled from motel to nursing home, and got very little from Ida that had not already been written. Then one day as she headed down the hallway and entered Grandma's room she found her sitting in her wheel chair looking out the window, with her hands clasped together in her lap; she had been crying.

Shannon just stood there for a moment. Then Grandma Ida said, "Come in, Shannon." Without looking back. "*How did she know I was there?*" Shannon wondered. "Good morning Mrs. Dawson." She said, "Everyone calls me Grandma Ida, I wish you would, too." "Thank you, I would like that very much," was the guarded reply. "Grandma, are you alright, you seem upset this morning."

Then the old woman said, "You know I have seen many of my friends die and I have outlived almost all my family, but it never gets easier. The woman who was in the hall the day you came died last night. She was ninety-one years old, I guess it was just her time, but it should have been me before her. I don't know how much more time I have left, here, but maybe God is trying to give me time for a reason. I have been an ornery old cuss and have chased a lot of people away who have wanted to know my story.

"My great grandson Charles came last night to sit with me for a while and we talked. He told me It would be a shame to keep all my history locked up inside and to take it to the grave with me, and not to tell anyone about our history and how we came to this valley. He said it was time for me to stop being so private and stubborn but to tell it like I remember it.

Charles Samuel Dawson is the only namesake left of our family. He was married once, but she couldn't be a rancher's wife so she left, before they had any children. He hasn't found another woman and don't know if he will, he is fussy about women, He says he is looking for another me.

I guess I should be flattered, but I wish he would find a nice girl and settle down and have the joy of having a family like the one I did, instead of looking for another me. There is and will only be one Ida Ingabar Lawson, Dawson. Isn't that a funny name? Lawson Dawson." Then she smiled and looked at me.

I said, "Grandma Ida, if I was to chose any other name for you I couldn't, it was made especially just for you, because you are unique and so is your name." Grandma smiled and said, "I have said more in the last couple of minutes then I have said in one breath for years. Maybe you are the one to write my story."

So began Grandma Ida's story. Shannon was to lose track of time over the next weeks. There were so many stories that came from her life, so many people who were involved in her life, and so many lives she and Charles Dawson touched. They weren't just one family of ranchers; they were "The family of all the ranchers in this valley." With some, they were the "only family." Over the next weeks Shannon felt like Grandma had adopted her, she didn't want it to end. She wasn't sure if their story even had an ending. When she called her publisher and told him she thought maybe she should rent a house here and plan to stay for a while, as Ida's story was not the only one to tell. Many of the old timers here had stories of their own to tell, and she wanted to hear them all, before there was no one left to tell them.

JOHN AND INGABAR LAWSON

Therefore, it began; Momma and Daddy grew up in a small village in Sweden and knew each other all their lives. Everyone knew each other. His parents were poor farmers raising six kids on a small potato farm. In the fall, they would dig up the potatoes and take them to the market in the town square to sell. They also had a pig and one cow, a dozen chickens that gave them enough eggs to feed their family and some for selling during the summer.

Daddy's name was John, he said he had been in love with Momma as long as he could remember; her name was Ingabar. By the time Daddy was nineteen and Momma was seventeen they decided they could make it on their own, so in a small ceremony at his parents' home they were married.

They set up housekeeping in a small dirt floor shack just down the road from Great Grandpa and Grandma Lawson's farm. They also raise potatoes, and Daddy had work a trade for a cow and some chickens. Try as they might, they just could not make a living. Then Momma found out she was pregnant. She told me it broke her heart when she lost their baby in the early stages of her pregnancy, but there was no time to dwell on it. They had to work hard to put food on their table.

Daddy said, one day he overhead someone on the street say

there was free land in America in the territory of Colorado, for people who were willing to work, and open up the West. He asked them about this land in America and how do you get some? They told him he would have to cross the ocean and go to the government office to apply for it.

Daddy ran home to Ingabar and told her about it and that he wanted to go to Colorado, America. He told her he was going to go see how much a ticket would cost them. She just stood there, he said, with wide eyes and her mouth open as if she was going to say something, but he didn't stop talking long enough for her to speak. Finally, he had to take a breath and she immediately put her hand over his mouth and said, "John, stop talking for a minute, and let me soak all this in. You want to do what?"

For most of that day, they talked about this free land in Colorado, America. They talked about how far America was, and where would they get enough money to buy tickets on a ship. Mostly they wondered what Colorado, America was like and could they grow potatoes there. One of the men he had talked to said something about high mountains, he called them Fourteeners. "What were they? And why did they call them the Rocky Mountains?"

It didn't matter and no one could talk them out of going. Momma and Papa Lawson tried their best, but in the end it was no use, so they said they would try to help them as best as they could, telling them if it doesn't work out they could always come back home.

John and Ingabar went to the land office and said they wanted to sell their farm and everything they had. They made a deal and were paid $500. They went immediately and bought tickets on the first passenger freighter leaving England. It cost them $200. They checked with the captain to see if there was a job they could do to pay for their room and board.

He asked them, "What can you do?" John said, "I am strong and will do whatever is needed," so he got a job shoveling the coal into the boilers. Ingabar said, "I am a good cook and I could help in the kitchen." However, he told her they already had kitchen help, but was she any good at cleaning? She said, "Yes." John said, "She always kept our house very clean." She was hired to do the housekeeping and to scrub the floors in the lower deck. They set sail in the spring. Everyone in the village was there to see them off, saying, "You come back if you don't like it there."

Grandma Ingabar was a small girl and no one noticed she was six months pregnant. She hadn't even told her momma. She wore her clothes very loose, and her apron hung loose around her tummy. The work she did on the ship was hard, with lifting the buckets of scrub water and mops. She was seven and a half months along when one night she went into labor. John wanted to go for the doctor, but she told him he would lose his job if he did.

By next morning their baby boy was born, he lived just a few minutes then he died. They named him Samuel Aully Lawson. John went to the Captain and told him Ingabar didn't feel well today and couldn't work, so the captain said she should stay beneath deck as not to alarm the other passengers. All that day she would hold her dead baby in her arms, singing lullabies and talking to him. John would sneak away from his job whenever he could to check on her.

By that night, they knew they would have to let their baby

Samuel go. So they wrapped him in the nicest small blanket and tied it tight around the bundle with cord they found and dropped him into the black water of the Atlantic, watching until they could not see the floating coffin any more. Ingabar turned her head into John's chest and sobbed as he held her tight in his arms.

The next day she was back at work, but by now, word had spread among the other house cleaners and workers about the baby, but it never went above the lower deck, code among the working class. What happens below deck stays below deck, but most of the other house cleaners and swabbers would walk over to Ingabar and take her mop or they would say, "I've got this room."

At first she would let them, but as she started feeling better, she would begin to carry her own share. These small acts of kindness was something Ingabar never forgot, and for the rest of her life she would find herself trying to pay back for it, by giving to others in their time of need. It took about a month before they finally made port in Nova Scotia, Canada.

After they landed and registered themselves with the Canadian Government, they traveled to the border of America, and registered again, there. They hadn't spent hardly any of the money they brought with them, they still had $276.37. They went directly to the Land Office, and to their surprise, it was crowded with other people looking for the free land in Colorado. They were afraid there wouldn't be enough for everyone, and it would be all gone by the time they got to the woman behind the counter.

They waited for hours, and then it was their turn. Two scared kids from Sweden, hardly able to speak English gingerly stepped up to the counter. The clerk looked up at them and said, “Looking for the free land in Colorado, would be my guess, huh?” They both nodded. The clerk said, “Alright then, name, where you are from, age and are you two all there is? No children?” Pause, and then they slowly shook their heads no.

THE LAWSON HOMESTEAD

The next thing they wanted to buy was a horse and a wagon, so they started looking for one, but they were in the biggest city they had ever seen and they were lost. They decided to go back to the land office and ask someone there about a wagon and horse. It was late and the office was closed. There were many people setting up a camp and staying there for the night, so they figured they would do the same. They did not have much, but they did have a blanket and their clothes, so being able to improvise they gathered some wooden boxes and made them selves a little hut to sleep in for the night. Others had already built their own and they would share whatever food they had with each other. John and Ingabar had taken some of the potatoes and beans from the freighter, and they were more than willing to share with these people.

They heard someone call their name and they recognized them from the freighter. They were headed for Colorado too, so they decided to tie in with them and go together. Next morning they all were in the land office trying to get as much information as they could. The lady behind the counter told them a man by the name of Jack Cord was taking a group of people west in a week, go see him and find out what he needs to let you travel with him and what you need for provisions.

Then the girl behind the counter gave them an address where he was staying. She also said something about learn to speak English and arithmetic if you plan to stay in America or else the criminals will cheat and steal everything you got, before you leave New York.

John and Ingabar had some schooling, but they were not fluent in arithmetic, so Ingabar asked the clerk how she could get a book that would teach her how to add and subtract. The clerk looked at her and then she said, "Wait here just a minute." She got up and left for a while and when she returned, she had a couple of books she handed to Ingabar. She said, "Take these and learn everything you can about keeping your finances accounted for. Write down every penny you spend in this column and every penny you earn in this one, and then in this column where you got it from and who you paid it to. Don't spend any more then you have and don't buy anything on credit, pay cash. Soon you will know how to add and subtract."

Then she nodded to the man behind John and Ingabar and said, "Next," and motioned with her hand for him to step forward. She smiled at the two young couple and said, "Good luck." She had no idea what her words meant to them, and over the many years they stuck to her advice to the penny.

For the next week, everyone was kept busy. John went to see the wagon master Jack Cord. He explained what their intentions were and that they didn't have much money. He must have been a real caring man, for he asked if John could drive a wagon and could Ingabar cook. John said yes to both questions. Jack said he had two boys and they were heading to Colorado also, but his wife had died and he needed someone to care for his boys and to take care of his wagon while he does the wagon master job. He would pay for the food and provisions. He had two wagons, but one of his sons was ten years old and could drive one of the wagons if John could drive the other. A deal was struck between them. John practically ran all the way back to Ingabar to tell her. Next day they were helping Jack get his wagon ready.

By the end of the week there were many wagons lined up in a big meadow in the center of New York. Everyone was yelling at each other and laughing. The horses were grazing near their wagons and children were playing in the big lake. Jack gathered everyone together that afternoon and as he stood on the back of his wagon he said, "I want to make sure you all understand, and I will only say this once, I am the wagon master, you will do exactly what I tell you to do. If there is any problem with that, do not come on the wagon train. This is not going to be an easy trip; there are no doctors, no stores, and no law where we are going. There will be bandits that will try to rob you and kill you for no reason at all, just to get what ever they can that's yours. There will also be hostile Indians so be on the alert, do not wander off by yourself at any time, keep your children close. Everyone has a list of the things you need, and number one is a rifle and ammunition. You had better know how to use it, because you do not want to waste any ammunition."

John looked at Ingabar with wide eyes and whispered, "I don't have a rifle." She said, "We will ask Jack where to get one." Jack also said, "Make sure all your wagon gear is secure and your wagon is sound. There will be no time to be fixing any wagons after we get on the trail. We will not wait for you. We will be leaving tomorrow morning at sunrise."

When he stepped down John went to him and told him about the lack of a rifle. "Gees, John didn't you think you would need one?" "I never thought about it," Jack said. "Come on we need to get you one. Do you think you can shoot one?" This was an after thought as he walked away.

By sunrise there was so much excitement among the people, they were all smiling and excited, yet there was tenseness among them, they gripped the harness riggings on their wagons making sure it was all the way it was expected to be. John and Ingabar were sitting together on the lead wagon, with Jack's son Joel behind with his brother Tad in the wagon.

Jack was on his horse riding back to check on all the wagons. When he came back to John and Ingabar he looked at them and asked, "Are you ready?" They both nodded. He yelled back, "Let's go." John lashed the horses and the wagon was moving, followed by forty other wagons.

Everybody yelling, "Hah, get going Molly, and get ups," all down the line. You could hear the whips as they lashed their horses, encouraging them to move. One wagon hadn't harnessed their horses securely and the animals left without them and their wagon. In a way it was comical, but their dream ended before they even got started.

As the days became weeks they traveled, filling their water barrels every time they were near the rivers and checking their food supplies. They were always repairing and making sure the wheels on the wagons were greased and tight. Jack told them there were a couple of wide rivers they would have to cross. The Ohio and the Mississippi, there were barges that would take them across, but it would cost more to get everyone across. He rode ahead and to find out how much it would be.

When he returned he told everyone it would cost them $10.00 each. Everyone argued, but in the end they agreed to pay, it was the only way across the river. It took most of two days to get all the wagons across. The barge could only carry two at a time, and there were other wagons heading for Oregon and California.

There was a land rush organized in Oklahoma about that time for free 160 acres. You had to line up and when the soldiers signaled to go, all the people who had a flag could race to a marker and place their flag in the ground and 160 acres was theirs. Many of the people in their train decided to go there. Now there were only twenty-six wagons headed for Colorado. John and Ingabar decided to stay with Jack as he was paying for their food and a place to sleep. They didn't have to spend any of their own money. They would need it when they got to Colorado.

They crossed the plains and once when they were on the plains they saw their first Indian. Jack went to talk to them and asked if they could just cross their country and if they could shoot a couple of buffalo as they were running out of food for the children. Jack had to give them ten of the horses first. The Indians said they would allow them passage as long as they did not stop. Jack said the group was only passing through. They left, but could see the Indians occasionally watching to make sure they did not stop.

During this journey, there was a woman who tried to teach some of the immigrants to speak English. John and Ingabar would study by candle light and they made a pact that they would only speak English to each other and practice. Finally, after three months they were in Colorado. Now they would have to look for a government office to see where the free land was.

In 1866 in the territory of Dolores, gold was discovered and there were many miners looking for gold and staking their claims at the land office. When they rolled into town with twenty-six wagons the miners yelled at them and told them to go back where they came from. They were not happy to see so many people coming, they figured these newcomers were prospectors, they never asked them why they were there. Most of these immigrants were just looking for farm land. They were known as "sod busters."

Jack came with all of them to help translate the paperwork they would need. They were shown a map and told to go farther west where the land was more level with less rocks and better for farming. Most of the people decided to take his advice. Nevertheless, John had noticed on the map a place in the mountains to the west where there were high meadows, much like the meadows of Sweden. He pointed his finger to a spot on the map and told Ingabar, "This is where we will build our home." She never argued with John when he made up his mind, just like when he told her, "We are going to America."

Jack told them, "I will come with you and help you get settled and build a barn." Then he would travel on west and see what was out there for him and his sons. Ingabar and Jack's sons stayed in the town of Colbran, while John and Jack went looking for the valley John had seen. Ingabar spent the time they were gone doing odd jobs for the locals and washing clothes for some of the miners. She learned she was good at making trades for food and merchandise. After three weeks had passed, Ingabar was becoming very worried when finally,

John and Jack came back, but they looked worn out, ragged. looking like they had been beat up.

When she asked what happened, they both smiled and said we had to build a road first to get the wagon through. Ingabar didn't even want to ask what they meant by that. She kept her thoughts to herself, but she couldn't help wonder just where their new home was going to be.

They bought more supplies of flour, sugar, salt and coffee. They bought traps and more ammunition, a few blankets and seeds for beans and potatoes. Ingabar checked their money supply and told John he would have to save some money for other things, and they had to pay $100 for the 160 acres to pay for the land. So far they had spent $79 and then another $10 for the barge to cross the river. They were down to their last $164.29, after he had bought the rifle and ammunition. Jack reminded him he needed a good saw to cut trees to build the barn.

The road to the valley was rough, and Ingabar was sore by the time they stopped. John came back to her and said, "My dear bride, this is our new home, what do you think of it?" Ingabar was amazed by the valley's beauty. There was a river running through the middle of it, with green tall grass growing on both sides, as far as she could see. There was a flat ledge to the right of the valley where John spread his arms to indicate everything and telling her where each building was going to be built. "We will build our house there, far enough away from the river so the spring thaws will not reach us, and the barn will go over there." Tall cottonwood trees lined the river, and in the distance high snow-capped mountains reached for the clouds.

The Douglas Fir Pine trees were growing almost to the top of the mountains. A couple of the mountains didn't have any trees on the tops. Jack said they were known as the "Fourteeners," and at 14,000 feet high, nothing grows that high. That night John and Jack had caught enough fish to fill their empty stomachs. It tasted delicious after the dry biscuits and beans they had been eating for the last three months. John was so excited he could not sleep. He talked most of the night keeping Ingabar awake. She finally just rolled over and let him talk.

Next morning John, Jack and his two boys started cutting the trees to build their barn. Jack had explained to them that the first thing you wanted was to have a barn for the animals to protect them from the weather. Without them you would not survive, the house would come later. For the rest of the summer they all worked hard. Ingabar would go out and find wild turnips and berries, she became very good at finding edible food for them. She dried everything she could, knowing they would need them for the winter. She got good with the rifle and would shoot wild turkey, and one day she even shot an elk. Jack had to show them how to skin it. He was skillful at drying the hide which Ingabar made into a blanket.

By the end of the summer, they had a barn built and that winter five of them made them selves a home in it, which they also shared with the animals. They now had four horses and six chickens, which Ingabar had bought after doing some work for a woman in the town of Colbran. She also did some sewing for a farmer and he paid her with a pregnant cow. She didn't know it was a longhorn breed from Texas. Ingabar told John the next time he goes to town he will have to buy a bull to keep her company.

The cow didn't like the confinement of the barn though and would tear things up inside their small house, on occasion with those long horns. On one occasion after Dolly (her name) had torn down Ingabar's clothesline she had strung across the rafters, John said, "It's time to evict our cow." It was kind of funny seeing Dolly there with Ingabar's undies hanging on her horns though.

That fall Jack and John would go out and hunt for meat. Elk and deer were plentiful, always bringing home one or two on a regular basis, to hang in their barn to skin. Then they would cut up the meat to dry over racks close to the fireplace. They had built the fireplace from the rolled rocks along the river's edge. Ingabar would use it to cook the meals. John had built a swivel iron bar to hang the pots on to cook the meat, and when it was done it could be swung out to serve food from the pot. They were all comfortable that winter.

When Christmas came they didn't have any gifts, but they had bagged a turkey and Ingabar roasted it over the spit in the fireplace, and then she made a berry pie. It was mouth watering good, and they were so happy with so little. Jack and John worked well together and Jack's boys were growing tall and strong, and helped out immensely.

They were such good help for Ingabar as well, now that everyone knew she was pregnant, they would spoil her, but she still worked just as hard as ever, even though John reminded her how fragile she was now. He worried about her. That summer they planted a huge garden of beans and potatoes, the soil was rich, and soon they had a large crop of beans to sell.

John and Jack took them into the nearest town with the beaver, muskrat and mink furs they had trapped over the winter. They traded for supplies and John thought that maybe he would see about getting another cow and a hog. He also thought he could get a cook stove for Ingabar to make her duties a bit easier. Ingabar remembered how her mother would make cheese from the milk they got from her cow. Ingabar would make cheese for them from any milk they didn't use and it was such a treat. The milk from these long horn cattle wasn't as rich with cream as the jersey cows she was used to in Sweden, but she made due with what she had.

Jack and his sons stayed on at the ranch for another year, helping John and Ingabar. When Ingabar went into labor that summer, John and Jack had to help with the delivery. Ingabar was in labor for hours and John was horrified that he would lose her, but the baby was a big healthy boy. They named him Lars Jackson after her father and they wanted to honor Jack so they added a middle name of Jackson. Lars Jackson Lawson sounded like a strong name for their son. By now they had constructed a small house, high above the river, and a well on the river bank built of rock and mortar.

The next spring, 1867 Jack told John and Ingabar it was time for him and his boys to move on. They saddled their horses and a wagon with supplies John and Ingabar insisted they take with them and after many hugs and Ingabar's tears they headed west. It was hard to see them go, but they knew he was anxious to start his own journey. He had said he wanted to go to the gold fields of Alaska. They wished him well, but they soon learned how isolated they were and how lonely they would be without anyone else around.

Over the years, they worked hard; they planted beans and potatoes, which they would haul into town to sell. John continued to trap for beaver, muskrat, and mink. They found the money they made on the furs was more than the vegetable sales. Their longhorn cattle had grown to a sizeable herd; they were a hardy animal and did not need much tending through the tough winters, but the meat from them was stringy and tough, not as good as the cattle they had had in Sweden. So John traded them and bought six dairy cows and one bull. They didn't fare as well in the harsh winters of the mountains, so John would bring them in to the small pasture near the barn, and feed them the hay he was able to store in the loft.

Ingabar had learned to make cheese from her mother and she would make the round cheese ball, and dip them in the candle wax to keep them fresh for sale. They became a very popular item in the grocery stores when they went to town.

She had two more little girls by now but one died in child-birth and the other (Ellie Sue) died when she was one. They named them Lillie Ann and Ellie Sue. They started their little cemetery on the hill under the big spruce trees and wild lilacs. John had erected a fence around it with a gate under an arch that read Lawson Cemetery. Ingabar would go there and place fresh flowers on the graves. On Ellie Sue's she had carved the words "Now God cradles my darling in His arms."

1878 a boy was born, Aully Mason, and 1880 Ida Ingabar. For the next years, there would be Laura in1884, and Maude was born in 1886. By now, the ranch was producing much of the valley's vegetables. Mostly root vegetables, like potatoes, carrots, turnips that faired the best. The quick growing vegetables like beans, peas, and cabbage would have to be picked and sold as soon as possible. Ingabar was well known for her cheese and it soon was in demand in all the stores in the valley.

John had to build a special room for her to churn and store it, so he built it of rock underground so it would stay at a cool temperature year round to age the cheese. The longer it aged the sharper taste it had. He had to make sealed containers to make sure the pack rats and mice couldn't get to it.

There was much to do on the ranch and Ida became very good with the cattle. There were no fences at that time so Aully would go out in the morning after the milking was done and stay with the dairy cows as they grazed in the high pasture. Then he would bring them back at night for the milking. Every day they would have to do this, and when Daddy needed Aully to help with something or to go to town to deliver vegetables and the cheese, which usually took a couple of days, Ida would take the cows out to pasture. She especially liked this. She had started to write poetry and this was a good time for her to write when she would sit under the tall pines and think and dream of all the things there were to do in this world. She was a dreamer.

One day while she was with the cattle, a young man rode into her camp. He was a handsome man in his early twenties. She wondered where he came from; she had not seen him in these parts before. He told her he had just come over the mountain from a small silver town called Crystal City. She didn't know where that was, but she asked him why he came here? He only said he just wanted to see what was on the other side of the mountain. She then remembered to ask what his name was. He said, "Charles Samuel Dawson," and then he asked what hers was. She said, "Ida." He laughed and said, "I like that name." She blushed; she wasn't used to talking to men, as there weren't too many who came to the ranch.

They talked for a while then he said he had to go into town to get more supplies, but he wasn't sure where or how far it would be. She said, "Just follow this trail it will take you to the Lawson ranch then you could take the road from there to town. It's about 20-30 miles down valley." He smiled and said, "I will be seeing you again soon I hope, Miss Ida."

That night she didn't say anything about the man in the forest, but at supper Momma mentioned a man coming to the house and said a young lady in the forest said if he followed the road it would take him to the town down in the valley. Momma asked Ida if she had seen him and she said yes, but he just asked for directions. She did not say any more. Momma said, "I fixed him a sandwich, because he looked like he hadn't eaten for a while." "That was nice of you, Momma." And after that nothing more was said about the man.

Lars had moved away from the farm, although there was still a lot of work on the Lawson ranch. Momma and Daddy couldn't hold him, so they gave him their blessings, and he found a piece of land down in the valley. Soon he had married and was doing very well growing crops. He planted an apple and a peach orchard that was thriving in that rich soil. Aully stayed on at the ranch for another couple of years, but he decided to head west to see what was out there. His heart was set on becoming a mountain man and wanted to explore the Rockies. No one saw him again for many years.

That left Ida the oldest now to help with the ranch. Momma had made sure every one of her children learned to read, write and learn arithmetic and to keep the money books. She kept telling us kids if you don't learn these things someone will steal everything you have, so every night before we went to bed we had to do our schooling. Ida had enjoyed that because she was doing some writing of her own and by now Momma had turned the finances over to her, so she kept the books and did a lot of the planting plans.

Momma and Daddy were getting on in years and Daddy was having trouble doing the hard work needed to keep the ranch going, so Ida thought maybe they should hire a couple of ranch hands to help. The next time Ida took a load of vegetables and cheese into town she inquired with the storekeeper if he knew of anyone who might be interested in a job on the ranch. He told her that he knew of one young man who had asked about a job awhile back, but he wasn't sure if he was still in town. She could check at the hotel. He said his name was Charles Dawson. So Ida headed over and asked if he was there. They told her to check at the stable, he was working with the horses and cleaning out the stalls.

Ida walked down to the stable and saw him in the corral; he was working a horse on a long rope, having him gallop around in a circle. Ida watched for a while as he brought the horse to a stop and had him facing him. He then motioned with his hand indicating for the horse to come forward. The horse acted like it was hypnotized, as it walked right up to him and nudged Charles in the chest. Charles rubbed his forehead and moved the mane off away from his eyes. Then he turned and said, "I knew someone was there, "Hi, Ida, how are you today." She was surprised he remembered her name.

She told him of her business and asked would he be interested in working for her family? He asked where the ranch was, and when she said, "I am Ida Lawson and we own the Lawson Ranch up in the high meadow." He looked down at his feet for just a moment then he kicked some dirt up, and then he said, "And, Miss Ida what would the wages be and what would I be doing?"

He didn't really care, as he had already made up his mind, but he didn't want to seem too anxious. He had thought about her since the first time he saw her two years ago. She told him, "Room, three square meals a day and thirty dollars a month in exchange for some really hard work." He said, "That sounds fair to me, when do I start?" She said, "As soon as you can get your gear together and get out to the ranch." He said he would see her in two days, as he still owed the stable a couple of days and he needed to settle up with the hotel for his room.

Daddy really liked the way Charles took over the chores and he was always very polite and helped Ingabar with much of the heavy lifting chores. Laura and Maude would joke that he was too handsome, and they would tease him about why he wasn't married. He just laughed with them, but he had only eyes for Ida, and as time past, they became close; they spent many hours fixing the outbuilding and working the beef cattle. They would brand and tag them, and when it was time to castrate the young bulls they worked together. Soon it became obvious there was more to Charles then just being the hired hand, Ida was falling in love with him, and he with her.

One night at the dinner table Daddy said, "Well Charles when are you going to pop the question?" Everyone stopped eating and looked up at Daddy in surprise, and then they all looked at Charles, he had just scooped a pile of potatoes on his fork and had it halfway to his mouth. He looked over his fork at Daddy, then he slowly lowered it and answered, "What question do you suppose that would be?" "You know durn well what question," Daddy said. "When do you think would be a good time, John?" "Well," Daddy said, "how about now?"

Charles got out of his chair and walked around the table to where Ida was sitting, spun her chair around to face him, got down on one knee and said, "Ida, this isn't exactly the way I had planned to do this, but here goes. I have loved you since the first time I saw you, will you be my wife? I will love you forever and I promise to be a good husband for you." Ida looked at him, reached out to touch his face and said, "I have loved you since that day, too and my answer is yes."

A loud voice from the other end of the table said, "Good, now that, that is settled, Momma, what's for dessert?" They all laughed as Charles kissed Ida. They were married in a small ceremony in the pine grove on the ranch, and then they left for a short honeymoon.

To their surprise Daddy had some of the other ranchers help him build a two-room addition on to the side of the house. It had an outside entrance so they could come and go without having to go through the main house. There was a bedroom and a small sitting room. Daddy had a small heating stove put in the sitting room and Momma, Laura and Maude had made a big oval braided rug for the floor. A couple of the women from town got together and made a quilt and two goose feather pillows for their bed. So when they came back to the ranch everything was ready for them. They set up housekeeping right away, but they still shared their meals together with the rest of the family.

For the next few years as Momma and Daddy got older, Ida and Charles took over most of the ranching. Laura got married and moved to town while Maude stayed on the ranch; she never married.

Charles Samuel Dawson, Jr. was born 1903; a Ute Indian woman was the midwife. Later after many years and many babies in the valley, everyone got to calling her Grandma Dandridge. She would make frequent house calls when she knew a baby was on the way. No one could say her Ute name, so she took the name, Helen. She told how a brave had kidnapped her from her village and traded to a trapper for two horses and had two children by him, and then one day he just left her.

When Charles found out about the Indian woman, who had been abandoned by her husband and was living like a wild animal in a cave with her two little boys, he told Ida about them. That night neither of them could sleep thinking about them, so the next morning Charles took three of their horses and went to look for them. What he saw made him sick. They had been eating roots and the mice raw that had been crawling in and out of the cave, when they could catch them. They were dirty and starving, and half frozen, they wouldn't have made it through the coming winter. He had some beef jerk, biscuits and some cider, and when he gave it to them to eat; they grabbed it and ate like animals. After they had eaten all he had, he put them up on the horses and brought them back to the ranch.

Ida had a tub of hot water waiting for them and with Maude's help; they gave the children a bath and cut their hair short to get rid of the lice and bugs. They had to use a strong solution of lye soap to kill the lice. After that, they applied a soft lotion to their skin. Helen had gone to the river and was washing herself there, and then she cut her hair as short as she could, they were covered with sores, and the lotion was a big help to heal them. That night they were fed a light supper as their stomachs would not be able to handle much.

In the meantime, Grandma Ingabar and Grandpa John were fixing up one of the rooms in the bunk house for them to live, and Charles was fixing a stove with a chimney and gathering wood. By the time everyone was finished, Helen and the children had eaten and were cleaned they were shown what was to be their home from now on. Helen was crying. She told Ida, "I will do everything and anything for you for as long as I live. I am indebted to you and your family for saving my sons' lives."

Ida told her, "Just live and raise your children, no one should have to live the way you had to. We are just glad we found you, I don't know how you survived as long as you did."

After everyone was settled in their beds Charles told Ida, "I need to go to the river and take a bath before I can go to bed." He took a big bar of lye soap with him and he was gone for a long time, but he sure smelled of soap when he returned. Everyone slept very well and at peace that night.

Maude took a great liking to Helen Dandridge and they would laugh and giggle all the time as they worked in the garden. Helen taught Maude to tan the hides from the elk and deer the Indian boys and Charles would bring home.

Ida would take her new son out on the horse with her whenever she went for a ride to check the cattle, and he would nod his head and say "giddy up" when he was put on the saddle. Most times, he would fall asleep before they would get back to the house, but he loved the horses and at a very young age, he soon showed signs of being an equestrian. He could ride just about any horse they gave him and it was his job to break them.

He had a gentle touch and could communicate with them. Soon the neighbors would bring some of the wild mustangs for him to break.

Their ranch was flourishing by now and they had enlarged their garden to an acre, they would grow beans, potatoes, squash, melons, pumpkins and corn, so they would have a lot of produce to sell all summer. They were able to sell the cheese year around. Ida told Charles, "I believe if we started making jerky we could sell it to the miners and trappers," so with the help of Helen and Maude they set up a smokehouse and would have a basketful of jerky to sell when they went to town, and along with the cheese they were able to have a year round income.

When it was time to butcher a hog, they would take the fat from the hog after they skinned him and slowly cook the fat in a huge iron kettle, then they would drain it through a cheese clothe. This made the best pure white rendered lard. After all the fat was drained, there would be a rind left and this would be made into Chitlings, we salted it and it was a good munchy snack.

A second son was born to Ida and Charles in 1906. They named him John William after Grandpa. He was a good baby and he would hang on to Maude's skirts and follow her around the yard; she would laugh at him and pretend to gallop like a horse he would laugh and run beside her. He was always happy and laughing. He gave so much happiness for John and Ingabar in their later years. John no longer worked the ranch, because of the arthritis, but Grandma Ingabar tried to help out in the kitchen and she still helped make the cheese.

Grandpa John died in 1913, he was buried in the family

plot on the hill, Grandma never got over the loss, and she died the next year 1914. They lay side by side for eternity. Charles made a cross and carved their names on it and he wrote an inscription that read, "In life they shared their love and in death they will forever be together."

The spring came and planting began; there were new calves and the herd was flourishing. Charles told Ida, "I think we will take a herd of the year old steers into town to the train station and sell them. It will give us a good start for the summer and we can get more seeds and supplies." Ida thought that would be a good idea, so with Johnny and Joel, Helen's two boys, Ida and a couple of the young cowboys, they had hired, Mac and Casey they rounded up one hundred and thirty steers. Charles told Johnny and Joel to stay with Maude and Helen and help get the field ready for the planting when they return in about a week, but to be sure to check on the cows that were ready to calve in the pasture.

Ida drove the chuck wagon with Charlie and Johnny sitting next to her, while Charles, Mac and Casey herded the cattle down valley the next day. It was a good day and everyone was in a happy mood. The cattle were sold at a profitable twenty five dollars a head. Ida did the shopping for their staples of flour, sugar, and coffee, while the guys took care of the cattle. She had wanted one of those new fangled washing machines that had a motor that ran on kerosene; she was able to get it loaded into the wagon and figured this would be the best buy of their trip. She could hardly wait to show it to Maude and Helen. Within five days they were all anxious to get back to the ranch and show everyone all the great things they had bought.

The closer they got to the ranch the more uneasy they

were beginning to feel, something wasn't right, there was no one coming out to greet them and no one in the fields. There was an eerie feeling about the place. Ida pulled up the reins and Charles told her to stay put, he will check it out first. He loosened his rifle from the scabbard on his saddle, as he slowly walked his horse to the house.

As he got off his mount, he saw Maude, coming from the bunkhouse, where Helen and the boys lived, she was pretty beat up. Her face was swollen, her mouth was bleeding from a cut and she was bruised along her arms. She had wrapped a scarf around her head, where it was obvious she had a large bruise. She fell into his arms, crying, "Helen is hurt bad, and the boys are gone." She sobbed. By now, Ida was running to the house. She grabbed Maude and said, "What happened?" Maude could hardly speak, but what little she said was enough. She repeated, "Helen needs you, He came just after you left "that trapper, Dandridge." He beat her and I think he violated her, and then he made me cook him something to eat. Then he said he was going to skin her alive.

"He had a knife and was trying to hang her up on the rafters of her bunk house, when the boys came riding back from the range and saw what was going on. They went crazy and started to beat him, I stepped in and everything got confusing after that, the trapper started beating on me. Then he ran outside and got on his horse and rode away towards the mountains. The boys went after him. I went to Helen and cut her down from the rafter, and then I passed out. I haven't seen the boys since, that was three days ago."

Maude took Charles' arm looking at him with tears in her eyes and said, "Johnny wasn't the Johnny we know. He had murder in his eyes. I am so afraid what they will do when they catch up to that monster, I fear for them, Charles, what are we going to do? I tried to stop them, but Johnny just pushed me aside and Joel said, 'I go with my brother, you take care of our mother. This hate has to end here'."

Ida asked, "Where is Helen now?" "She is in the bunk-house," was the reply. Ida asked Maude if she was all right and did she need anything. She said, "No, go to Helen she is really bad hurt." Ida and Charles ran together to the bunk house, and found Helen lying on her bed.

Her face was hardly recognizable from the swelling, there was a rope hanging from the rafters that had been cut where Maude had cut her down. There were dark blue bruises around Helen's neck. Her eyes were no more than slits from the swelling. Ida for the first time in her life swore, "That son of a bitch, he needs to be killed, he is nothing more then an animal, after all he has put this poor woman through, he needs to be killed." She immediately began to swab Helen's face with a cool cloth. Maude said, "I have tried to help her, but she doesn't really know that I am here." Ida told her, "You did well, but you also need help."

Charles had taken the children off the wagon and taken them to the house so they wouldn't see this, while Casey and Mac unloaded the wagon. Then Casey rode to the next neighbors to get help, and In the meantime Charles was saddling a fresh horse. He asked Maude which direction the boys had gone. She told him towards the high meadow where they had found Helen and the boys in the cave. Ida came outside and told him, "Don't bring him back alive."

Charles had never seen that look in her eyes before, but he

knew what she meant. He took her in his arms and said, "My love, I promise he will pay for what he has done to our sister and to Helen and the boys, but for now I have to find Johnny and Joel before anything bad happens to them. They are our boys and if he gets to them before I do, I don't know what he might do to them, they are so young."

Mac went to his Charles and asked if he wanted him to go with. He said, "You best stay here with the women they will need all the help they can get, son." Ida packed him a bag with food to last awhile, and then she kissed him and he rode off with a very determined and worried look on his face.

The neighbors came to help, each one taking turns sitting all night with Helen, until finally after four days she started to wake up and respond to their nursing. The ranchers helped get the garden plowed and planted. It had been three weeks and Ida could hardly think straight, she would walk to the edge of the hill watch the horizon and waiting, she must have said a million prayers at that time. Then off in the distance she saw three horses and riders. She let out a yell for everyone to hear and ran halfway down the pasture. Charles had gotten off his horse and met her half way down the meadow. "I was so worried." Then she loosened her hold on him and went to the boys crying, "My boys, I am so sorry about all this." They looked at her, and Johnny spoke first. "Momma? How is Momma?" "Oh my God. I'm sorry, she is going to be alright, she will take a while to heal, but she is strong and she will be fine."

They didn't hear anymore as they raced for the house. As they burst into the room where she lay they knelt by her bed, she looked at them with eyes still badly swollen and bruised, but was unable to speak with her broken jaw, it had been bandage closed so she couldn't move it, but she held her hands out to them and tears rolled from her eyes. She had so many questions.

Then Joel leaned close to her ear and whispered, "He will never hurt you again, it's over." She looked at her son and blinked once as to say, she understood. Ida asked, "Where did you find them? What about the Trapper Dandridge?" Charles looked at her and said, "This will not be told to anyone, it is finished. He will never come back again, and He can never hurt anyone again," and with that he walked away. Somehow she didn't need to know. He walked down by the river and washed his face and hands like he just couldn't get the dirt off.

Johnny was a changed young boy after that. Before he always was quiet and kept to himself, he had so much pain and hurt inside of him he couldn't let it go. Many times Ida noticed he would be staring in the direction of the old cave. Once she walked out to him and asked him what he was thinking. He would just say, "Nothing," and walk away. No one could reach into his thoughts, he was in his own world, and he never smiled. After Charles brought them back to the ranch he sat next to his mother he laid his head on the edge of her bed and cried for the first time. Helen placed her hand on his head and said in a whisper through her clenched teeth, "It's over my son, it's done, cry it away," and together they cried.

After that Johnny was more alive then he had ever been. He would join in when the family got together and he would even laugh when they joked. He especially liked playing with the children when the neighbors would come to visit. All his pain had vanished, he was a sweet loving son to Helen and even

Maude, who was his favorite person, he would tease her and they would laugh together.

Later, after she had healed from her injuries, Maude took the rifle and the .45 pistol from the mantle, and went to Charles saying, "I have never liked the idea of guns, but I have thought about it a lot these last couple of days. I figured there is a time and a place that they are useful for many things. I will never be this vulnerable again. "I want you to teach me how to shoot one or both of these." Charles looked at her and said, "I would be honored to teach you." In the next few weeks he would take her out into the far woods and set up targets, and then he showed her everything there was to learn about shooting a gun.

She got so good at it that most times she would go out on the hunts with the guys and always bagged an elk or a deer. One time she even shot a mountain lion that was after a young calf. The guys would ask if Maude would come along to be their guide, and when they knew she was coming they knew there would be meat for all to share. Soon she would hire herself out as a hunting outfitter. She and Charlie would set up a camp for big city hunters wanting to have a rewarding hunt. They paid well for their services, because they knew they would always get an elk or deer.

When Ida would say we need a chicken for supper tonight, Maude would grab the rifle, go shoot one in the head and bring it into the scalding pot to be plucked and cleaned. In those days when anyone got an animal it was shared with all the neighbors, and even after the state decided there had to be a hunting season, there was a lot of poaching. The game warden's job was a dangerous one, a couple wardens just didn't come back, and their bodies would be found in the spring. When a hunter did shoot an elk he would bring it to the Dawson Ranch to hang and skin. The meat was cut up and divided to many of the families around who were less fortunate than the ranchers.

The game warden would come to the ranch, but most of the meat was already cut up and either dried or wrapped and in the root cellar to keep cold. He never inspected that area, and didn't even know it was there. Ida would always make sure he took home a good chunk of her cheese. That always made him, "look the other way."

1917 America was at war in Europe and Laura's husband insisted he should go and fight. She begged him not to go, that he had a family, but she couldn't stop him. By 1918 she received the letter from the War Department that started, "We regret to inform you and, so on," She came home to Charles and Ida, with her family.

They made another room in the bunkhouse for them. Their home now consisted of fourteen people, so Charles, Charlie, Johnny and Joel, and the two ranch hands, Mac and Casey went to the forest and started cutting logs to build a bigger bunkhouse with an extra room for a bedroom in each apartment. They had no idea how much use these little bunk house apartments were going to be in the future. Charles and Ida's house was a two story frame house, and their children and Maude would live there with them, but Helen, Johnny and Joel had their own house, and now Laura and her two children had a place and the two cowboys had a place of their own.

About this time Maude decided to have a small cabin built for her near the river, she would have many of the neighbor women come and together they would make beautiful quilts.

When Maude would go to town, she would be sure to pick out new fabric. Mostly she would buy blue and white, as these were her favorite colors. When the ladies could, many of them took old jeans or denim and cut them in long strips and braided them together to make into big oval rugs. It was always a busy and happy time. Maude would make everyone laugh with her happy sense of humor, and she would bake sweet treats for everyone, to serve with her special mint tea.

There were still four more rooms that were empty, but somehow Charles thought the way their family was growing he just figured a couple extra would be a good thing and they could use them for a tack room and workshop and now they had eight rooms.

Ida had two more children, daughters Virginia and Elizabeth. That next winter was an especially hard one, the snow started and the wind would blow endlessly and didn't seem to stop, some times the drifts would reach the top of the windows. It was hard to keep a path shoveled from the bunkhouse and the barn to the house. They would tie a long rope from the house to the bunkhouse and then to the barn to follow during the blizzard that had become so often this winter. Charles worried about the cattle and could only hope they had found some means of protection from the snow and able to forage for some grass. They had put up enough hay for the dairy cows, but there wasn't enough to take to the pastures for their range cattle.

Spring was long in coming, but it finally did come. The melting snow from the mountains caused the river to raise higher then usual, making it was hard to get across to check on the cattle. One time Johnny tried to cross the river but the soft mud and the current pulled him down with his horse. Johnny was able to get himself out of the mud and swim to the opposite shore to Maude's cabin. Maude took him in and got him out of his wet clothes and sat him by a roaring fire to warm up.

She fixed him a hot cup of soup that she always had going on the stove for the guys after they had been out on the range. Then she ran to Ida's and told them what had happened and told them Johnny's horse was stuck in the mud and couldn't get free. Mac and Casey grabbed a "Snatch block" from the tack room and headed for the river. The horse was able to get himself across the river but got stuck in the mud on this side. He was up to his belly in mud, it was obvious he was just about worn out and was giving up.

By now, Joel had arrived to help, and together they had wrapped the rope around the horse's neck and around his belly; they attached the snatch block to one of the big cottonwood trees, and when they would smack the horse on the rear and it was just like pulling dead weight. The horse had no more fight in him. So they had to use drastic means to get him to help and to fight, so Joel would straddle the horse and push his nose under the water till he couldn't breathe, and then he would rear his head out of the water and lunge forward, at which time Casey would pull on the Snatch block and they would edge forward a few inches. After about an hour of this inch by inch progress they finally hit some solid ground and the horse was able to help himself out of the mud. Mac climbed on his back and ran him up the hill to the barn. The horse was trembling and so weak by now, but Joel took him into the barn and rubbed him down with gunny sacks, making sure to rub his legs to keep them from tightening up till he quit quivering, and then he fed him a good bucket of grain.

No one knew just where the measles came from, but it soon spread like wildfire; there were no ranches that hadn't been affected by it, and the small children were dying, and they didn't know how to stop it. Ida heard there was a vaccination they could get, but only the people in the town were given it, as the doctor wouldn't or couldn't get to all the ranches. When Charles and Ida's daughters got sick and after Laura's little girl died from the measles, Charles decided to take matters into his own hands.

The very same day he contacted a couple of other ranchers and they went to town looking for the doctor. By the next morning, they rode into the town of Colbran and asked the doctor to come with them and bring all the serum he had. They would make sure he was taken care of and they would bring him back after he gave all the children vaccinations. He said he couldn't do that, he was needed in town. Charles said, "You are also needed at the ranches, there are children who are dying there from this measles epidemic."

When the doctor insisted he couldn't leave, Charles turned and walked outside the doctor's office. He knew he had to calm down as he was mad enough to shoot someone and told the other ranchers what the doctor said ,and then he said, "I don't want you all to get into any trouble on my account, but I do not plan to go back home without the doctor and the serum."They didn't have to think too long when they said, "We will go get his buggy; you fill his doctor's bag with as much serum as he has got, and we'll be back in ten minutes."

Within fifteen minutes they were all on their way out of town with the doctor in the buggy gagged and tied to the seat, his doctor's bag was packed full of as much vaccine and medicines as he had. That little doctor's buggy never went so fast before, hitting just about every rut in the road, it was a good thing the doctor was tied in his seat or he would have been thrown out. The ranchers wasted no time getting back to the Dawson ranch; every ranch family within ten miles was at the ranch, ministering to a sick child. The doctor was pretty banged up after that ride, but he started to give everyone the vaccinations. He looked at Charles and said, "I may as well check everyone else over, as long as I am here, looks like I won't be going back to town unless I do, ain't that right, Charles?" "Yup," was all Charles said.

Every room in the bunkhouse was full of people as it had been made in to a hospital. Maude was cooking soup for everyone and Helen was handing out the hot bowls. Johnny and Joel had the awful job of digging graves, there were already four children dead, and Ida's two little girls were just barely alive, she was by their side, holding them close to her. She looked up at Charles when he walked into the room, and said, "They are gone, my babies are gone." He knelt and wrapped his arms around all three of them and held them close to his chest, and wept.

The vaccine was working almost immediately, but for some it was too late. Eight children had died; they were all buried on the hill in the Lawson cemetery. Charles and Ida told everyone, "This is our family cemetery and we are all family."

The sign was changed after that and below the original sign it read: The Dawson City Memorial Cemetery. From then on anyone who died on the mountain was buried there, and after the years it expanded and a bigger fence was put around it.

Lilacs and blue spruce trees were planted, flourishing. Every spring the lilacs would spread a sweet fragrance that filled the valley.

In the fall, the ranchers would always come to the Dawson Ranch for the annual harvest celebration. There would be fresh vegetables, Charles would butcher a steer and have it roasting on the big rotisserie spit. Charlie would go out and get the steer he had been fattening up with the corn stocks from the garden, making it sweet, juicy and tender.

The night before a big pit was dug and Manzanita wood had already been cut and gathered for the pit; it was lit that night so the coals would get red hot. Charles and Charlie would be up before dawn getting the carcass wrapped with burlap and wrapped in place with bailing wire. All the boys would take turns turning the spit to keep the temperature all the same to cook evenly. The Jackson ranch was busy roasting a hog, in a buried pit in the back yard, and all the women had been cooking and baking all week. Everyone was looking forward to this all year, they had all worked so hard and lost so much this year; they needed to have something happy to think about.

When the wagons started showing up and all the greetings were shared they put their food on the long table Johnny, Joel and John William had built. They also made long benches so everyone could sit at the tables together, as they wanted to be close to each other, they needed the family closeness this year.

There were a few people who had walked to the cemetery and were walking among their family members' markers. Soon everyone was gathering there. Ernie Jackson was the Preacher whenever there was a need for one and he said, "Let us all hold hands bow our heads and say a prayer for the ones that are not here in person, but in spirit they will always be with us." They held hands and formed a circle that wrapped all the way around the cemetery. "Father, we come to you as a family," he began, and when he finished everyone said in a loud voice, "Amen."

Then they ate till no one could eat anymore, they talked about children, crops, cattle and hunting, they laughed and told old stories. The children played games, but many would sit and listen to the older folks talk. Many set up camp in their wagons and some slept on the ground, but no one was anxious to leave. They were neighbors enjoying each other. The Jackson family played music and everyone danced till late into the night. There was a huge harvest moon that lit up the entire valley that night. It was so beautiful it was a perfect night to remember for the rest of his or her lives, but reluctantly two days later everyone left.

Charles and Ida were sorry to see them go, but there was work to be done and they had a wagonload of squash, melons and potatoes to haul to town to be sold. Meanwhile, Charles and the other ranchers started to round up the cattle for branding, before they took them to the cattle yards.

Ida, Maude and Helen thought it would be a good time for them to take it in, they needed to shop, and they hadn't done anything like this together before. So after everyone helped load the wagon they were off to town. It was an easy trip and they sold everything they had on the wagon. They set up their camp along the river, and then next day they went shopping for supplies and fabric. They were having so much fun they didn't notice an old bearded man watching them.

He was dressed in buckskin with a fur hat and well worn

boots. He was pretty unkempt looking, but there was a familiarity about him. Maude was the first to notice him and when she told Ida about him, she too thought she had seen him before, but couldn't recall where. Finally he crossed the street and walked up to them. They were surprised when he spoke. "I would know you in a crowd, Ida and Maude Lawson, I don't know this young lady," he said, indicating Helen, "but she sure is pretty little thing," and then he laughed. "Oh, My God," was Maude's shocked reply. "Aully?" He smiled that wide smile they all knew. Ida and Maude grabbed him at the same time hugging him and asking questions at the same time. He laughed and said, "You have to be careful with me, I am an old man now remember? I will answer all your questions, but first I just want to look at you."

He said, "I had wanted to come back to the ranch to see Momma and Daddy, but I was either up in the Rockies trapping and hunting for the big resort folks or hunting for gold in the Oregon and California gold fields." He had even gone to Alaska and was a Royal Canadian Mounted Policeman, for a time but grew tired of the cold winds there. He got lonely and had a hankering to return to the ranch in Colorado. "I asked about the Lawson Ranch, but everyone said it wasn't the Lawson Ranch anymore it was the Dawson Ranch. So which one of you is the Dawson they tell me about?" "That would be me," said Ida. "My husband is Charles, and I want you to meet him."

After some more shopping, they left for the ranch the next day, with Aully on his Bay Stallion following behind. Ida laughed and looked at Maude and Helen and said, "We might have to build another room on the bunkhouse." Aully was happy to be back home. He pitched in with all the chores and fit right in with everyone. He would tell them stories about his travels and he said he had kept a journal ever since he left the ranch; he had to practice his schooling as Momma told him to.

Maude and Aully would walk out to the cemetery and look down at all the markers. He said, "One thing about a cemetery, it holds a lot of history, someday it should be told." Maude told him, "Momma missed you so much; she spoke of you all the time, wondering if she would ever see you again." He very quietly whispered almost to himself, "She will very soon." Maude looked at him with the look of puzzlement. He looked at her and said, "I have that disease they call cancer, and only have a few months left to live, but I don't want you to say anything to anyone else though."

Maude kept her word and didn't tell anyone, but she spent as much time with him as she dared without raising suspicion. He died that fall and was buried in the family cemetery, next to Mamma and Daddy. One day a week or so later Maude went into Aully's apartment to clean it out; when she noticed his saddlebags leaning up against the wall in the closet. She picked one of them up and opened it.

On the top was a white linen cloth, and as she unwrapped it she found the white hanky she had give4n him just before he road away so many years ago, with the names sewn into the corner, MAUDE AND AULLY. She held it to her lips and kissed it so tenderly. Then she noticed the journals, and as she took one out, she noticed it was dated 1900. She opened it and started to read, but quickly closed it, feeling like she was invading a very private thing. So she took them back to her room and for a long time she would look at the saddle bags, but she remembered what he had said at the cemetery, "History should be told or it will be lost forever."

Aullys Journals started, "Aully Mason Lawson, born 1878, on the Lawson Ranch, on what was known as The Grand Mesa in Colorado. Maude kept the diaries to herself until her death, where Ida found them among her things. They were along with her own journals tied with a blue ribbon and wrapped in a silk scarf and placed in a hope chest full of all the things she never got to use for the husband and family she never had. Ida took the journals and placed them back in Maude's hope chest. It was many years later before she would open them and read their stories.

SHANNON

Shannon had decided living in a motel while writing this article on Grandma Ida wasn't very practical. She thought she was just going to write a short little article and that would be it, but there was so much more to Grandma's life that needed to told. The thought of a novel grew in her mind, as she began to think about the lives the Dawsons had touched. There was Aully and she began to realize Maude had a story to tell. What happened out there in those mountains with Johnny, Joel and Trapper Dandridge?

She needed more room to spread all her papers out and a lot more privacy. Maybe even a telephone would be nice. There weren't too many apartment buildings in Dawson City for that, so she decided to go talk to Lorrie, maybe she could help her.

Next morning she got up early and went to the nursing home so she could have a few minutes to talk to Lorrie. She saw her leaving one of the rooms; and as she was shutting the door behind her she saw Shannon standing there. "Good morning, Shannon, You're up early. I don't think Grandma is awake yet." "I didn't come to see Grandma; I came to see if you could help me." Then she told her what she needed, and Lorrie told her, "Give me a little while and I will check on something for you."

Later that morning, there was a knock on her motel door,

and when she opened it Charles was standing there. He wasn't dressed in his suit and tie like before, but he was in jeans and a blue cotton chambre shirt, looking much like a working cowboy. He had his Stetson hat pulled down over his forehead. He was so handsome standing there; she just stared at him like some silly schoolgirl. Then he said, "I hear you are looking for a house to rent." Finally she was able to speak, and she said, "I think it would be better for me to work, it's a bit too noisy here and I could use a little privacy."

She wondered, *"Why does he have to be so good-looking and sexy? He must think I am a real ditsy thing, I'm so tongue tied whenever he comes around me. These goose bumps, what's with that? I've been around men before, for crying out loud."*

"I think I might have just the right place for you. Get in," he said as he opened the door to the passenger side of his old jeep. He took her arm to help her in, and then he walked around to the other side and got in. As he turned the key in the ignition, the motor started with a roar. They backed out of the drive and drove about a block, and then he turned into a short driveway lined with blue spruce trees on each side. As they drove up to a little cabin that looked like it was as old as the mountains, she noticed the flowers that well groomed and the small lawn gave the smell of just being mowed. The porch stretched the full length of the front of the cabin, with a swing attached to the rafters and a cushion on the seat. Next to the door was a polished oak rocking chair that over the years had been well.

Charles got out of the jeep, and walked around to open her door. "Come on, Shannon, I think you will like what you see inside." She was staring at this beautiful storybook cabin. Then she said, "This is so beautiful." He just smiled. They walked up the steps and as he opened the door, she passed in front of him. She stepped into the small room, stopping and looked all around her. The Bay windows overlooked a garden in the backyard where hundreds of rose bushes and lavender flowers, lining a stone walkway leading to a carved wooden bench, overlooking the river and the meadow on the other side. White lace curtains with pearl tiebacks adorned the windows. As she let her eyes wander around the room, she noticed the small kitchen. Everything was done in polished pinewood. The countertop was smooth polished stone, looked like it had been specially sanded from the round river rock, with pebbles inlaid between each rock, and several layers of clear lacquer covering them to protect the surface. There was a round dining room table with four chairs all in the same pinewood as the cupboards; each chair had a little blue and white checkered pillow on the seat. The furniture was all primitive hand made and polished to a shine.

In the cozy sitting room, there was a desk with a desk chair near the windows, and a small settee against the wall with a matching chair facing it. A miniature coffee table between them was covered with a hand crocheted doily, and on the floor was a round braided rug that someone had made with much loving care. It looked like the fabric was from wool shirts and denim jeans that had been cut into strips and braided, then sewn together and made into a circle just big enough for the sitting room floor. A tiny fireplace was built into the corner so it filled the corner and faced the room.

The bedroom had a full size bed, with a lace skirt under the mattress that touched the floor and lavender and blue handmade quilt over it, with two matching lace pillows leaning against the headboard, a crystal lamp was sitting on the nightstand next to the bed.

The pine dresser with washbowl and pitcher sitting on the top looked like it had been made by hand and a full size mirror hung against the wall. There was a music box sitting on the side, and off to the side was the bathroom with just a shower. There wouldn't have been room for a tub. Next to that was the closet.

Charles watched her as she wandered through the house. He was feeling the presence in the room, he could feel the life that had lived here and the love that was still here among all the lovely things. It had been a while since he had opened these doors, but he had made sure it was always kept clean and the gardens were always maintained.

"What is the story of this amazing gem?" she asked. "It is so beautiful." "This is Maude's home," was his reply. "No one has lived here since she died. Everything is just as she left it. It is yours to use as long as you want to." Shannon turned to look at him; she was surprised that he would allow her to stay here. She thought she heard a bit of tear in his voice. She said, "It is so beautiful and it feels so warm and soft, if that's the right word." He knew what she meant, as he felt the same way about this house. "It needs someone to live here, that can love it the way we do, and I think you are the right person for that.

Maude would very much approve, she was an amazing woman and there is no way this cabin should be kept hidden away like it has been, but it needed the right person." Shannon said, "I would be honored to stay here, I will contact my employer and he will send you a check."

"Shannon, you don't understand, this place is not for rent.

Maude would not approve. It is yours to use as long as you are here. She was a very giving person and would never ask for anything from anyone, she would invite you in as her guest, and that is what I am doing for you; you are a guest of my Aunt Maude's." All Shannon could say was, "Thank you, I will cherish this house and I wish I could say thank you to Maude." Charles smiled and thought to himself, "*Maude heard you*." Everyone said Maude's spirit never left this house. Even the woman who comes and cleans has said she felt Maude's presence here and sometimes finds herself talking to her.

Shannon was so anxious to move in here and knew she should call her boss, but decided not to right away, as she did not want to lose this wonderful feeling she was experiencing.

She spent most of the day getting her things hung in the closet, spreading all the material she had gathered on the small table so she could get it typed and sent to her office in Denver. By that evening she realized she hadn't eaten all day, but just as she was about to go to Dottie's for dinner, Lorrie drove into the driveway and told her she was invited to her house for supper. She wanted her to meet her family. Shannon was more then happy for the opportunity to eat something other than the rich food from Dottie's restaurant.

Spending time with Lorrie's family that evening was nice. She had a very amiable cowboy husband and two energetic boys six to ten years old. They would run around wrestling and playing with the dog, but when she said it was time, to eat they would sit down and their manners were impeccable. After dinner, they would help their mother clear the table, before they left to go back outside, as they still had some chores to do helping the father with the horses.

Shannon said she would wash and Lorrie could dry the dishes, as she knew where everything went, but Lorrie told her the boys would do them in a little while. They have chores in this house like everyone else. We don't discriminate women work here, it's everyone's job to work in the house and do outside work. Come I want to show you our ranch. "Shannon," she asked, "Can you ride a horse?" "Yes, I used to ride all the time when I was at home with Dad and Mom." "Good, let's go riding; I think I have a pair of riding boots that will fit you."

When they got outside there were two horses already saddled and an old man with a big old well worn hat and wearing faded blue jeans that looked like they had seen their better days, was leading them over to Lorrie. He said, "I figured you would want these two fellas." Lorrie said, "Thanks, Dad, you know me too well. "I want you to meet my friend Shannon; this is my father, Joel." Shannon looked at him; somehow, she knew he was "The Joel" that Grandma Ida had been talking about. He was dark skinned and quite obviously an Indian. She said, "I am so pleased to meet you, Joel," as she reached out her hand. He looked at it then he reached out and took her into his arms. "A hug is better don't you think?"

They rode for about an hour as Lorrie explained every detail of the mountains, and as they galloped across the meadow heading for home, Shannon felt at home, she was happier than she had been for a long time. When they got back to the house the kitchen was all cleaned up and there was a roaring fire in the fireplace. Her husband asked if they had a good ride, Shannon told him it was so beautiful. He just smiled.

That night she slept so peacefully that she woke with a start, wondering where she was. She lay there and looked around the room, not wanting to disturb this moment, it was such a peaceful place, but it was time to get this day started. She had some writing to do and maybe she should go get some groceries, and maybe she should call her boss, or not. A lot of "shouldas," but she couldn't care less for the moment.

For the next couple of days she checked on getting a telephone, did her laundry, organized her story, but she hadn't gone to the Home. She figured Grandma might need a rest after all the information she had already given her, besides, she just wanted to stay in this house, and she felt so at home here.

She looked at all the pictures hanging on the walls and was intrigued with the ones of Maude and her children from the school. Maude was a petite woman with the prettiest white hair, and she had such an infectious smile. There was one where all the children were surrounding her and they were in a "Big hug." There was one that must have been taken years ago where she and an Indian woman were hugging each other and smiling as if they had a private joke between them.

Shannon looked at all of them they were mostly of family. She recognized Grandma Ida, holding hands with two small boys. The one looked like Charles when he was very young. One picture in particular caught Shannon's eye though. It was of a very handsome young man sitting next to a young Maude. He had his arm around her shoulders. It was obviously taken at one of the hunting camps Maude used to ramrod in the mountains. It was signed "Lovingly Yours, Mitch."

This was a home where family was a very important part of Maude's life. She was smiling in all her pictures and the people she loved always surrounded her. "I wish I could have known you," Shannon said aloud as she touched the face of the lovely woman smiling back at her in the picture. Just at that moment she felt a cool breeze brush past her, and she thought she felt a light touch on her shoulder. She looked up, but there was no one there. Shannon smiled, as she remembered what the housekeeper had said, and then she whispered "Hi Maude."

About three days had passed and she still hadn't called her boss and she had not gone to the home to see Ida. She finished writing and had her story caught up, but she had spent a lot of her time sitting next to the water watching the rapids as it twisted and turned around the rocks. She could smell the lavender flowers and the roses as the breeze sent their fragrance her way, they intoxicated her.

That was where he found her. Charles walked around the outside of the house, and when he saw her he stopped to watch her a moment, he thought she was so beautiful sitting there. Then he softly called, "Hi Shannon, I knocked, but there was no answer, your car was still in the driveway, so thought I would take a chance that you would be out here. This is where I could always find Maude. She loved to hear the water and smell the flowers." "Oh, Yes, I can believe it, they are intoxicating."

"Charles, tell me about her, she must have been someone very special." "She was," he said as he sat next to her on the small bench and their legs met. "I can't tell you much, but when I was old enough I spent most of my time with her. She would tell me stories about the hunting camps and about the mountains and the animals. She would say, 'Never shoot an animal unless you are in danger or it was injured and needed to be put down, or you need it for food, and always respect them, as they are the most beautiful creatures God created. She kept journals of her life but Grandma has her journals, and they are so precious to her, I'm not sure she will share them, she has only let me see them once, and she cried that day, but she wouldn't let me take them home to read. It was as if it kept Maude close to her and she didn't want to lose that. Someday I will see them, but for now I'll just wait."

Shannon then asked about the picture of Maude and the man names Mitch. Charles smiled and said, "Maybe he was special in her life, but she only had him in her hunting camp for three years. He would come from Chicago, and they would spend every minute together, but then one season he never came back. For a long time she was very depressed, but she never spoke of him again, and no one asked her about him. Only once did I hear her say something about his wife didn't want him to come back to hunt. Soon after that she quit doing the hunting camps."

Shannon asked why he was here. He said, "Well first I just wanted to see you and find out if you needed anything. I went up to see Grandma last night and she said she was worried about you, she hadn't seen you for a few days."

"I'm so sorry," Shannon said, "but I figured she needed a rest from all the interviewing. I will go see her tomorrow."

Charles said, "I have a better idea, Grandma does have a day out once in a while, so why don't I come pick you and her up, then take you out to my ranch for a nice lunch tomorrow?" "I would like that very much." "Good, then I will be by about 10:30 to get you, and together we will go pick up Grandma."

Grandma Ida was dressed and ready for the ride to Charles' ranch when they got there. He gave her a hug then she reached out to Shannon and gave her a hug. Shannon felt so close to Grandma. Maybe she was letting herself become too attached to this family, but for today it wouldn't matter, she was just going to enjoy everyone and everything. Charles was so gentle when he placed Grandma's arm in his and walked her to the car, this time he didn't have the jeep. He was driving a well polished 1980 black Cadillac Seville. Not what Shannon would picture him driving.

The day was spent talking and laughing and telling stories. A very nice older woman served lunch on the veranda. There was lot of fresh fruit, served with a fresh chicken salad, and delicious homemade bread, warm from the oven, and a small dish of strawberry ice cream and cake for dessert. Shannon hated to see this luncheon end; Charles' house was so lovely and tastefully furnished with polished wood and leather furniture. There was a cowhide rug in the middle of the floor. It was definitely a rancher's home, but it was also a home a woman could live in and love.

It was time to take Grandma back to the nursing home; it was obvious she was getting tired. Charles asked her if she would like to lie down in the bedroom for a while, and he would take Shannon for a tour of the ranch. She said that would be perfect, so he took her to a very nice room and helped her into the bed and covering her with a blanket. Then he told the woman, who served them lunch to keep an eye on her, and that nothing else needed to be done but Grandma Ida for now. She nodded that she understood.

Charles and Shannon walked out to the lawn and he showed her all the flowers and told how they were taken from the seeds of the original flowers planted from his great grandmother Ingabar's garden. There were lavenders and roses, blue, pink and yellow ones that lined the walkway. Shannon asked if he did all the gardening, and he laughed and said no. He didn't have the talent to do that, he has someone else do it for him. He had all he could manage with the cattle and the ranch.

He showed her the stalls where some of the most beautiful horses were stabled. He raised Quarter horses. Then he showed her his stallion and he gazed at him with a lot of pride. "I raised him from a colt and now I am about the only one who can ride him, but he has sired some excellent foals." Then he took her for a walk to the pasture that reached to the far grove of pine trees. There were about 40 Black Angus grazing in the tall grass. It was a post card picture. He told her the rest of the cattle were up in the high country for the summer, but in another month, he and his wranglers would be bringing them down. They would be branded, and then they would drive some of them to the railroad down valley. Some would be taken to the stockyards, but most of the cows would be taken to his ranch down in the valley for the winter, where in the spring they will calf and then be brought back to the high pastures. She was amazed at all this and couldn't get enough of all he was telling her. She wished she could be here to see it all, but she didn't tell him that.

She said, "I didn't think how much work there was involved in running a ranch." He said, "There is a difference in just running a ranch and running a ranch like a business. There is a lot of paperwork involved, explaining some of it to her. Then he stopped and said. "I'm sorry, Shannon. "I'm sure this must be pretty boring for you."

Shannon said, "No, no I think it is very interesting, and it is very obvious you love what you do. That is rare in this day and age. Most people think of their jobs as a thing they have to do day after day. It's rare to see someone body so passionate about it, I envy that." Then she looked away and gazed at the beautiful scene in front of her. He wondered about her story, and someday maybe he will ask, but not today.

When they took Grandma home, Shannon told her she will come by tomorrow, if that would be okay with her. Grandma Ida took her hand and said, "I would like that, very much." Charles leaned down, kissed her on the cheek, and said, "Goodnight, Grandma." Lorrie took her by the hand and asked, "Did you have a good day, Grandma?"

She said, "It was lovely," as they walked away.

"Thank you, Charles, I can't remember the last time I have enjoyed myself so much." He said, "We will have to do this again soon." Then he bent and kissed her cheek, "I will see you soon." She smiled and knew she wanted that very much. She knew also that there was more to the way she was feeling about this man than she wanted to admit.

GRANDMA IDA PART 2

Grandma seemed anxious to get started on her story again, so starting was no problem. Shannon didn't want to wear her out though. Grandma asked, "Now where did I end?"

By now, WW1 was ending and soldiers were coming home, a few of the ranchers' sons came back pretty emotionally battered, but given time they were able to salvage their lives and get them back together, but those that came back in a flag draped pine box were buried in the Dawson Cemetery. It took a few years for the parents to accept their loss, but the thing about these people was they were tough, and they knew they had to move forward. James Clemens was never able to accept the loss of his only son and he was found hanging from the rafters in his barn. He was buried next to his son in the Dawson Cemetery.

Everyone was either working their cattle ranches, some even started to raise sheep and was grazing them in the high country during the summer months; it would cause some problems with the cattlemen. They said the sheep eat down to the roots and it leaves nothing left for the cattle, so there was a meeting and the ranchers and the sheep men divided the area. The sheepherders would use the east side of the mountain and the cattlemen the other. It worked out real good that way. Everyone had to work together to survive in this wild country and on these mountains.

One time the sheepherders had a hard time getting their sheep down from the mountain, as the Mexican help decided they would go back to Mexico, and fight in their revolution for their country. Therefore, the ranchers said it couldn't be that hard to herd a bunch of stupid sheep, so they offered to help get the sheep off the mountain. They found out sheep didn't herd like cattle and it was a comedy to watch.

Sheep were going one way and the cowboys the other and horses were bucking, as sheep ran under their bellies. The herders were running all around telling the cowboys to get off their horses and get them under control. I think there might have been some choice words that mountain had never heard before. The sheep and cattle were all mixed together and they didn't like each other much, eventually they all were herded into the meadow below. However, herders and cowboys had quite a work out that day, the one thing they all agreed on was, "They wouldn't try that again."

They all had a big party on the Dawson Ranch with one roasted sheep and one roasted calf after everything was sorted out. They were laughing and teasing each other about all the things that happened that day. They joked that maybe they should trade, the cattlemen would shear the sheep and the herders could castrate the yearling bulls.

It went down in history as the "Biggest Sheep Rodeo" of all time. All anyone had to do was mention the "Rodeo of 1920" and it would bring a smile and a laugh to everyone's face. Then the stories would start all over again.

Those next years were all about getting the ranches going, raising children and the Dawson Ranch was soon becoming the place to go for everything. It was actually becoming a town more than a ranch. A sawmill was started up valley near the timber. Maude decided there were many children in the area so she started a school, in no time they had to build a place for it, as the ranchers were anxious for the children to learn their reading, riting and rithmatic. The three R's they called it then. So the neighbors got together and cut the timber and took it to the sawmill having it cut into lumber, and then they built a schoolhouse. They built the foundation out of the rolled rock from the river. When it was finished, there was enough room for about thirty children.

During the winter when the snow got too deep for the ponies, Ida and Charles fixed up the bunkhouse for the outer area kids to stay for the week, and then they would go back to their ranches and help with the chores. The ranchers' wives would fix food and bring it to Ida to cook for their kids' meals; the children would cut wood and keep a fires going in the school and in their bunkhouse rooms. They were also required to make sure there was plenty of firewood for the main house. The girls would help with the cooking and cleaning up. These were good kids and they knew how to work hard.

Eventually there were some of the Ute Indian parents who wanted their children to learn to read and do math, but they couldn't speak English, so Helen started to teach them to speak English and she taught the English-speaking children to speak Ute. Not all the children liked the arrangement of sharing their bunk rooms with Indians, but after a couple were told they couldn't be there if they didn't learn to get along and were sent home, they figured it out and learned to tolerate each other. Their fathers gave them a good lesson in getting along when they heard about the "little" fight that happened one night, where much of the furniture in the bunkhouse was busted up. I don't know too much about that lesson, but a couple of the Indian boys and a few of the white boys had a hard time sitting down for a few days. In those days, discipline was tough, and fathers gave out the discipline with a belt. The boys had to build new bunks and stands, as well as fix the stove they had knocked down. Ida made them wash the walls from the chimney soot that was spread all over the room. The boys especially didn't like the first night after the ruckus, when they had to sleep in a cold bed, while their blankets were drying in the house. There were no more fights and they quickly learned to be friends.

Someone started a general store, and stocked it with many of the staples they needed, like flour, sugar and coffee; otherwise, they had to go all the way to Grand Junction for their supplies. These supplies were brought up be truck now, as the motor age was here. Flour, sugar and salt were a very important commodity for everyone. Most of the folks had their own meat. In addition, they still would go out in the high timber and bag an elk or deer on occasion

When the stock market crash happened in 1929, at first it didn't really affect them as most of them were self sufficient. However, unlike Charles and Ida who had the ranch free and clear of any debt. There were ranchers who still owed a mortgage, and then when the banks closed and they had to sell their cattle or sheep to make their payments, eventually they were so far in debt they lost everything. Charles and Ida bought a couple ranches by paying off their mortgages, in the lower meadows where the heavy snow and subzero temperatures, didn't affect them and it would be good grazing for the cattle during the winter months. These ranchers had planted peach orchards on their property, so Charles arranged with them to stay in their homes and take care of the orchards and he would give them a share of the profits when it was time to harvest. Ida suggested they put in a produce garden in the lower end of those properties, where there was good water drainage. They thought that was a good idea, she explained it would make an income early in the spring and they would have that all summer to sell. The "Share Tenant Farmers," were more then happy with this arrangement.

There were other ranchers who had nowhere to go and their children were obviously starving. Helen knew how that felt and she asked Ida and Charles if there was something, we could do to help them. These children would come to school without having eaten since the day before.

They would sit in the class and stare at the blackboard, but unable to concentrate, they were just too hungry to think about school, but it was warm and that was all they cared about, and they knew they would get dinner at noon.

Ida had been so busy she didn't know just how bad it really was for the other ranchers. So one day she had Maude, Helen and a few ranch hands come with her while she went to a couple of the neighbors to see for herself how they were making out. What she saw made her heart hurt. Most of them were trying to keep their households going, but they were holding on by the tip of their fingers. The fathers were trying to get work wherever they could, but most times, they would come home with nothing. They would dig in the garbage of others to bring home some food for his family. One woman had dug up some wild turnips and that was all they had to eat.

One time while Charlie was staying at the store he had fallen asleep, and awakened by the sound of something sliding off the shelf, so he quietly slipped into the store area thinking it was a pack rat and noticed a man he knew filling a sack with food. Charlie knew this man and knew he had five kids and they needed food. So he stayed hidden and kept track of what was put into the sack, after the man slipped away into the night, Charlie figured how much was taken, put his hand into his pocket and counted out the cost and put the money into the cash register. He never told anyone about the intruder and never let on to the man that he had seen him. He did see him later and just treated him the same as before.

Some of them had to butcher their horses for food. These were their neighbors, and Ida couldn't let this happen to them, so that night she sat down with Charles, Maude and Helen. As they sat around their table, her boys and the other ranch hands had come into the house. "What ever was going on?" they asked. "We think we should know, because this was all our business too and it would affect us.

Their son, Charlie said, "Mom you always said when we put in that cemetery that it belonged to everyone, because everyone was family here in this area, and we can't turn our backs on our family." Ida was speechless, she was so proud of her sons, but today more then ever. They were no longer children, and they understood.

So as everyone talked about what they should do, it was late into the night before a real solution was reached. Next morning the men got to work with the boys from the school who were big enough to work hard.

Next to the school, they built a large building with rooms

big enough to house at least four or five small families. The neighbors came as soon as they heard what was happening and pitched in with what they had left to work with, and within a month, the two-story house was built, with two rooms on the lower level and two on the top. There was a fireplace in each room, it would be up to the families to furnish them, but for now, they had a roof over their heads. They would bring whatever they had with them and pens were built for any animals they might have had. There were chickens, goats, cows, rabbits, and many horses, which were put out to pasture. One man brought a long horn cow, but having heard the story of Grandma Ingabar's Long Horn cow it was decided this one would make a very good meal for everybody.

Soon every room was filled, and everyone would help hunt game to feed everyone. Ida's small kitchen was always filled with women cooking and canning or drying meat. They would work together, no one ever had a bad word for the other, which could have turned into a bad thing, but they would teach each other ways to fix something out of nothing and nothing ever went to waste. Ida thought maybe if anyone had a recipe for goat cheese. They could make some and sell it in the valley. It was a good idea, and they made many pounds of it and could hardly keep up with the demand.

One lady told how her grandmother, who came from Sweden, after butchering chickens, would keep the feet and scald them in boiling water long enough so the outer layer of skin would peel off. Once they cleaned it off, she would simmer the feet in chicken broth. Then she would make a milk gravy and place the feet in it and serve it with boiled potatoes. They tried that and there was such rave response about how good it was, and asked for it all the time. One of the women had a recipe for soda crackers, another for a "Poorman's Cake."

A couple of the women were teaching the girls to cook and one woman was a seamstress and would give lessons on her treadle sewing machine; the girls would soon be making their own clothes and soon they became very good at it. Men would show the boys to do carpentry. One man who was taught by his father to build furniture was setting up a small space in the barn to teach his craft to the boys who were interested. Some of the girls would make cushions for the chairs. Others were ranchers and the one thing they knew how to do was handle cattle, there were some pretty good cowboys who came out of those years.

Soon we were having rodeos on the ranch, the women would make money selling their baked goods and by now, the peach orchard was thriving, and Saul Johnson would bring up a truckload to sell along with some of the melons he had grown in the garden.

So many good recipes came from the Depression, Grandma Ida said, "I wish I had written them all down." We all worked hard, but together we survived. We didn't take the commodities that were handed out by the government; we were a community of survivors. There were a few who gave up and left, and there was one killing over a deer that was shot with one man claiming it and another saying it was his, no one won from that. They could have just split it in half, but I guess when you have a family to feed and you're hungry you don't think straight.

I lost John William in 1941, he was driving a herd of cattle to the train yard in Grand Junction, when they stampeded during a dry lightning storm and he was caught in a small canyon where they ran him over. This was a low time for me. Now I only had one boy left, Charlie. If I would have lost him, I don't think I could have survived. I had five children in all. My heart was broken when they brought his body home. My neighbors did everything they could to comfort me, but I have learned only time will heal the loss, but you never forget the giving birth of a child and all the love you felt for him.

Shannon waited for a few minutes as she saw the tears in Grandma Ida's eyes, then she knelt beside her and wrapped her arms around her and they cried together. Ida said, "It was so long ago, but it feels like just yesterday, He was such a joy."

In the 1930s President Roosevelt decided to put together a program to try to get the economy back on track, they called it the construction years.

They started the WPA and the CCC better known as the Civilian Conservation Corps. Several names for the same thing. It was designed to get the people back to work and the nation back on its feet, and it did. They were building damns and roads, and reservoirs. They had one started in the Durango area, they called the Vallecito Reservoir. It was to supply water irrigation to the Ute Indian ranches first, and then to the white farmers.

It was a huge help to control many of the flash floods that ravaged that area from the snow melt in the spring. Some of this construction had to stop when the Japanese bombed Pearl Harbor and the United States went to war with Japan December 7th, 1941. Helen's sons Johnny and Joel enlisted.

It was all we could do to keep Charlie from going. He had a wife by now, but when we explained he was the last and only one left of our bloodline, they gave him an exemption. He felt he was letting his country down, but we needed him on the ranch, and besides he was thirty-eight years old then, I guess they took Johnny and Joel because they weren't married and did not own a ranch.

Helen was so worried, many nights she would walk the meadows and one time we found her chanting in the old Ute ways, praying to the Great Spirit. We all prayed with her in our own way and when the paper came and it read like Laura's husbands did, "We regret to inform you and so on." Helen was devastated and inconsolable.

Another letter came shortly after that from his commanding officer, "your son died in battle having risked his life in the line of duty. If it weren't for his heroism, a full platoon would have been trapped and all would have been killed. He has been awarded the Medal of Honor from his country that he so gallantly gave his life for." His body was returned to Dawson City to be buried, with a full Honor Guard.

Many soldiers and families came for the service from the surrounding ranches even some from Grand Junction, the Ute Indian Tribe came dressed in their native dress. The chiefs wore their long Eagle Featherhead dress. The military gave Helen the folded American flag and the Ute Indians gave her the eagle feathers of the warrior.

Before the ceremony was over a big black sedan drove up to the cemetery. When the door opened Joel stepped out, there was such a loud cheer. Helen's legs gave out from under her and if it were not for Charlie and Maude, she would have fallen to the ground. She regained her strength, ran to Joel, and collapsed in his arms crying. There wasn't a dry eye in the entire crowd, including the soldiers with the rifles and the honor guard.

Joel told later that when the news got to him about Johnny. He went to the commanding officer and told him about Johnny saying, He is my brother and I have to go home to my mother, she needed me there, I am all she has."The Commander called the Pentagon and told them the situation. "This was the brother of a Medal of Honor winner who was killed saving an entire platoon.

It did not take much time for the paperwork to go through, a special plane was ordered for him and he had it all to himself. A car was waiting for him as soon as he stepped off the plane, he did not even have time to think. They told him he was registered in the nicest hotel in Honolulu, and they would be there the next morning at 0600 to take him to the airport.

Everyone in the lobby had heard about him and his brother and they would come up to him and hug him and say how sorry they were and they would pray for him and his mother. There was a car in the morning to take him to the airport and another one when he got off the plane in Denver, Colorado. They drove him from there to Dawson City, stopping once to have lunch.

The letter came from the President of the United States that read, "Your son will remain in history for all to see for as long as there is an America. We are proud of all the soldiers who fight for freedom, but one such as your son will never be forgotten. We honor him. My sincerest condolences for your loss, Your President, Franklin D, Roosevelt." A huge marble headstone was erected at the gravesite in his honor. At first, he was going to be buried at the Arlington Cemetery, which was for the heroes of all the wars, but everyone in the area fought to bring him home to his own land where he was born. Finally the military consented, but they insisted on a large marble stone be placed there to honor him. It read: Johnny Dandridge: Medal of Honor: Died serving his country beyond the call of duty: WW11 1943: DOB Unknown

Someone had scratched into the stone, "Our son has come home to us, and His spirit will always be among these hills."

All of these things to honor our son were very nice, but it didn't fill the emptiness we all felt. The war was over for Joel, but he had to deal with the terrible things he saw and the loss of the brother that he had loved so much, they had endured so much together. A few years later Joel did marry a nice girl who had two of children, who were also left fatherless because of the war. They had a daughter of their own, and they named her Loraine, but everyone called her Lorrie. Charlie also had a son born in 1947; He was named after his grandfather and his father, Charles Samuel Dawson the Third.

By now the civilian construction boom had started up again and the Bureau of Land Management was looking at the Dawson Valley to put in a reservoir. This could not happen here, there was too much history and so much living that went on here.

DAWSON RESERVOIR

The fight to live in Dawson City was to begin a completely new meaning of family and home for all the residents of this valley. For the next four years, the nation would know what the American Spirit could endure. There were wars where soldiers fought hand to hand and died protecting their homeland, but now they would see how far the pioneers would go to protect their "home land." They did not arm themselves with guns; they armed themselves with knowledge and determination. They did not have the "big shot lawyers." They had only an army of people who were not going to go down without a fight, they had one Native American Ute Indian called Johnny or better know to his people as Chief White Feather, who were not going to yield to government bullying, and that was a powerful army.

The Bureau of Land Management and the Water Conservancy Co. were just as determined to have the valley for their reservoir. They stopped looking anywhere else and wouldn't consider an alternative.

The government officials from the Bureau of Land Management and the Water Conservancy Agency came to the ranch and tried to talk, what they called, "some sense" into this stubborn old rancher and his feisty little wife, but to no avail, neither would yield.

One day a black sedan, with government license plates

on the front with a couple of men in black suits carrying brief cases stopped and got out of the car. As they headed towards the front door, Charles met them before they reached the first step. They tried to introduce themselves, but before they spoke, he told them, "Don't waste your time introducing yourselves as you won't be here long enough to matter and I'm not interested in your names or your business."

They said they only wanted to talk for a few minutes. He said, "State your business, because a few minutes is all I have time for." They told him they understood how he felt, but the reservoir had already been engineered and this was the best place for it, then they showed him the plot map. Charles looked at it, and then he said, "Do you realize this will take all of my grazing land, my house, the school and all the buildings on the ranch, not to mention the cemetery."

With that Ida, who was standing next to Charles placed her hand over her heart, she softly whispered, more to herself then aloud, "Oh my God, this isn't possible."

Charles said, "No, we will not leave this ranch."

Then the two men said something that Charles could not tolerate. They thought they could threaten him, when they said, "You will have no choice, either you go willingly and be compensated for your land at fair market price and also enough for you to move, or we will move you by force and you will get nothing."

Charles saw red, as he took a step closer to them and said, "I want to make this damn clear and don't be mistaken; we will fight you with all we have even if we are left with nothing, we will not go down without a fight. This is our land, we worked for it and our mother and father homesteaded and worked hard for it. We will not give it up to a bunch of government bullying or threats. This ranch is still ours now you have used up your minute, now I will give you about one more minute to get off our land before I go get my shotgun and show you how we deal with threats."

They knew he meant business and as they turned to leave one of the men turned and yelled over his shoulder saying, "We will see who leaves, and this is not over."

Ida looked at this husband of hers and never felt so proud in her life, but with a quivering voice she asked, "What *are* we going to do?" Charles watched as the car sped away kicking up a cloud of dust. He said, "I don't know, honey, but I do know we have to fight."

And fight they did, even the neighbors who had ranches below them had been visited by these officials, and some of them were ready to give in to their demands, but a few of them said they would not move. Orey Jackson, who had the ranch about three miles below The Dawson Ranch, was at home when the black shiny car drove into his driveway, but before they got out he stepped in the front with the shotgun pointed at the front window of their car. He told them not to get out of the car, but to turn around and leave or he was going to make a sieve out of their car. They did as they were told, and left in a cloud of dust.

Several of the ranchers and their wives went to the Capital in Denver; they talked to the Governor, but found him to be a little worthless person. How he got to be Governor was beyond their imagination, all he could tell them was they would have to go to the Bureau of Land Management and the Water Conservancy Agency and talk to them. They tried that, but they would not listen, they just told them they could go to the President of the United States for all they cared, it would not change a thing. Their plight was in all the papers, they decided to get a petition for everyone to sign. They had 10,000 signatures and they took it to the senators who were supposed to represent them, but they didn't really want to get involved.

The ranchers were just about at the end of their rope, they did not know where else to turn. It looked like they were beaten. Charles, Ida and the other ranchers had sold most of their cattle to fund this fight and they were out of money.

It had been three and a half years and they were no further ahead, they had put up a good fight, but they were facing defeat. Charles and the other ranchers decided to go see just how many cattle they had still in the high country. Therefore, they organized a roundup and left one morning in August.

Ida and a couple of the other wives were sitting on the front porch, not really talking, just looking out over the meadow and watching the river, when a cloud of dust indicated another car coming up the road. I do not think I can talk to one more of those assholes from the BLM or the WCA. I think I will just get the shotgun and shoot a hole in their rear ends. All the women laughed, but they knew what she meant. They had felt the same on many occasions.

However, this time it was different, the nice dark blue shiny sports car did not have any official looking government license plates. It said Native American on the front. A tall impressive handsome Indian stepped out of the car. He stood and walked with great poise, his head high and proud as he slowly walked up to the steps. He noticed the pistol Ida held in her hand, and some how he knew she wasn't afraid to use it if necessary.

She said in a stern voice, "Now what do you want?" He put both of his hands up with the palms facing her, and with a slight sign of a smile he said, "I am not your enemy, I have come to help you." He felt great admiration for this warrior woman. So he continued cautiously. "My name is Johnny White Feather and I am the Chief of the Ute Nation from Utah. I have come to find my sister, Bird Who Flies, you know her as, Helen Dandridge, is she here?" After what happened to Helen with the monster trapper Dandridge every one in the valley was especially protective of Helen.

"How do I know this is true and what do you want with her?" "I do not blame you for your distrust and you protect her well and that is good. She was taken by a brave from our village many years ago and traded for ponies to a trapper, by the name of Dandridge.

"My father searched for many years and he died without knowing where she was or if she was even alive, but before he died he forced the brave who traded her, to tell him what he had done with her. After he told Father, the brave, "was no more." By then all, the tribe was sent to reservations in different places and our father had to give up his search. When we heard the story of the Warrior Johnny Dandridge and his mother Helen Dandridge our hopes came back to us, much has kept us from searching any more, but now I am able to come. I long very much to unite with her and to see her and the children she has left.

For a while, Ida looked this tall Indian over before she turned and called to the boy who had been carrying in wood for the kitchen and told him to go fetch Helen. He ran as fast as he could to the school, as he burst into the school, he yelled,

"Helen you have to come to the house, there is a big Ute Indian Chief there to see you."

Before she could say anything, he dashed back out the door running for the house. He wanted to see this Indian some more. Helen turned to the children and told them to continue with their work. No one was interested in his or her schoolwork, even Maude had stopped with her students. She told them to stay and do their work as she ran with Helen out the door. There was no way those kids were going to stay and do their work; they all were out the door as well heading for the house.

Helen got just about halfway between the house and the schoolhouse when she stopped. Johnny White Feather turned and smiled, He started to walk towards her with his arms out stretched, He said, "My sister, Bird Who Flies, but he called her in the language of the people. She covered her mouth with both hands. "Oh, My God," she cried, then she ran to him,

"I didn't think I would ever see you again."They held each other for a long time. They looked at each other, "There is so much to tell you," he said. "There are so many questions." She took him to her little apartment and for the rest of the day they would talk and they were seen walking along the river and across the meadow.

Finally, Ida called to them saying, she had supper ready and would they like to have something to eat. At supper that evening, he told of how the Bureau of Indian Affairs had taken many of the children from the reservation, cut their hair, and forbid them from talking the old language of the Ute Indians. After they cut their hair, they tried to turn them into white children dressing them to look like the other children of the white settlers and for some this was okay, but our mother and father insisted we stay with our tradition. In secret, they would make me practice our ways. Although the schools of the white people were good, and I learned much there, but I still practice and I prefer our old ways.

The Indian agencies would pick children who had excelled in their teachings, and send them to higher schools. I have been in Washington D.C. practicing the government legal system and have read everything I can about the land disputed. I thought it would help our people on the reservation.

When I read about your valley and read about Johnny Dandridge and my sister "Helen", I knew I had to come here. I have done much research; and I think I know a way for you to keep this valley and the Dawson Ranch or is it Dawson City? Either way let me tell you what I have discovered.

That night all the women stayed and sat around the large table listening, without interruption to Johnny White Feather talk. He spoke very eloquently and in simple language, they could understand. They felt he was talking to the councils of his fathers.

He began, "I want you to understand in order to present this to the Congress of the United States and that is where you will have to begin. We will have to have all our 'ducks in a row,' so to speak. There can be no loopholes for them to tangle up against you, and they will try.

"They also know the right words to use to confuse you." Laura sat there with intense interest and wrote down everything he said. They were up until late into the night talking and asking questions.

Finally Ida said, "Maybe we should sleep on this and let this poor man get some sleep as well." He nodded and said, "I am very tired, I have come a long way."

Helen said, "You can sleep on Joel's bed." The other women stayed sleeping wherever they found a space, mainly on the floor with a blanket. No one wanted to miss one word of Johnny White Feather's talk.

Next day after breakfast, they made a plan, now all they had to do was present it to their husbands, this was to be their last stand and it had to be good.

The next day the men brought the herd into the lower meadow; there were only about a hundred and fifty head of fat beef, belonging to everyone. This was all they had left of the two thousand they started out with that spring. You could see the despair on their faces.

They did not know what to make of this tall Indian, who was sitting on the steps of the porch. Charles spoke first; he was not in a very good mood when he asked, "Who the hell are you, another Government man?"

Ida came out the door before Johnny could speak and said, "Charles this is Johnny White Feather Chief of the Ute Indian Nation from Utah, He is Helen's brother and he has something all you men should listen to, He has come to help us keep our land."

After all the men had eaten and heard what Johnny had to say, Jackson, another rancher said, "We have just brought in the last of our herds and it will not amount to much if we have to go all the way to Washington D.C." Charles said, "I don't think we really have a choice Jackson, this will be our last chance, and we have to try."

Money was a great concern, everyone had used about all

they had and were down to their last cent. They had hoped for better results, hoping there would have been more cattle. How were they going to raise any more money?

Then one of the women said, "You know that rich woman from down in Grand Junction has always wanted to buy the brass bed that was my mother's. I could sell it for some money." Another woman said she had some work she could do as well and sell things at a stand at the swap meet in Grand Junction too. The women and the children at the school could make quilts to sell also. Even some of the furniture the boys had built had to be worth something.

This went on for a while. They all wanted to do something, so they got busy and made a plan for all the ways they could make money to finance the trip to Washington D.C. They had a huge swap meet in town and many people from Grand Junction and surrounding areas came. Everyone had heard what they were doing and everyone wanted to help. By September 1, they had raised enough for tickets for eight people on the train.

It was all set, Charles, Ida, Laura, Maude, Jackson and his wife, Carol, and Emil and Cali Mason, were the eight who it was decided would go.

Johnny said he would not accept their offer to pay his way; instead, he would pay for both his and Helen's tickets. There were ten people in all going to see the Congress of the United States. Laura had struggled over what to say, and she wrote a speech, but none of it sounded good enough to plead their case, and she knew this was their last chance, so it had to be good.

The trip to the capital in Washington, D.C. on the train

seemed like it took forever. They had packed enough food to last a week and they would get together in the dining car setting out their food on the table, eat and talk. The other passengers would stare at them, but they did not care what anyone thought, they only had just so much money and they had to be careful how much they spent. They did not know how long this would take and they still had to come back.

Laura spent a lot of time alone trying to write her speech, she was so scared. She felt everything would depend on her. Charles walked in on her, finding her crying. She had a pile of wadded up paper where she had thrown it, He did not have to ask what was wrong, he knew. He just did not realize how much this meant to her.

He took her in his arms and said, "Laura, you cannot let this get to you, no matter how this turns out, good or bad it won't be because you did it wrong. We are in this together, and we all have done the very best we can, there is just so much we can do. If we lose Dawson City then we will do something else, but we will all do it together, that's how we have always done it and that won't change, that's how we will keep doing it." He pulled her away from him and looked into her face, wiping the tears with one hand. He continued to say, "Mom and Dad Lawson came with a promise of free land, which turned into a homestead. Then it became a ranch and finally the City of Dawson, everyone in the valley made it possible, we have memories they can't take away, and that is what we will take with us.

Now I want you to leave all this here and come out and join all of us. We might as well enjoy our selves; none of us have ever ridden on a train, so let's just consider it an adventure."

He stood and reached for her hand and together they walked out to the dining car. The rest of the evening, they all laughed and exchanged old stories. The kind that started with, do you remember when...? Then they would all laugh. Other people in the car would listen to them and soon every one was sitting around listening to them. Johnny White Feather sat and listened to all these stories and he could see how much these people had been family. He admired them for their perseverance and the love they had for each other.

When they walked into the halls of Congress, Charles in his suit looking so handsome, Ida in her homemade dress, looking so pretty, everyone had on their best clothes, but compared to those people in their smart tailored suits they looked like country folk, but none of this would matter after today.

Laura and Johnny White Feather stood and waited to be announced, and then they proceeded to the table in the middle of the room. The man sitting up high, looking down at Laura and Johnny, behind a long table with other stern looking men leaned into his microphone and said, "Please states your name and your business." His demeanor said, "Let's get this over with."

Johnny stood up and said, "I am Chief Johnny White Feather of the Ute Indian Nation and I represent the party from Dawson City, Colorado. They are here to ask your help to stop the Bureau of Land Management and the Water Conservancy Agency who want to build a reservoir on their land and flood their homes and their ranches. Mrs. Laura McCoy would like to speak to you and tell you why they want this not to happen. They had been fighting this for three and a half years and have had no one that was willing to listen to them." Then he stopped talking and waited.

The Speaker of the House asked as he looked at Laura, "Mrs. McCoy, would you please stand and state your case please." Laura stood and stepped to the podium and began. Thank you, gentlemen, I am not an eloquent speaker, so please bear with me as I speak in the only way I know how. I am a rancher's daughter, and I would like to tell you about Dawson City how it came to be.

Mamma and Daddy came to America from Sweden with a dream. They had heard of the free land that was being offered to anyone who had the determination to face extreme hardships to help open the Wild West. They were two young kids, Momma was seventeen and Daddy was nineteen

They landed in Nova Scotia in 1865 and came by wagon train to Colorado. By that time they had lost one daughter in early pregnancy and a son who they had to bury at sea, before even touching foot on land, but they would not give up. Daddy had to cut through forest and move rock to build the road to the meadow he had picked out for their farm. The meadow would become Dawson City. When the Homestead Act came into affect, they paid $100.00 for 160 acres. It was called the Lawson Homestead. They spent many years building their ranch alone but eventually other ranchers came and built their homes further down valley.

They suffered freezing winters, starvation, extreme isolation and the fear of Indian attacks, but Daddy went to the village of the Ute Chief Ouray and they talked. Daddy told him he would give his tribe two cows every year in the fall if he would let him stay there and could keep his home. They agreed and it was settled, by smoking the peace pipe. There was no war and no danger of any attacks.

One especially hard winter two braves came to our house and gave Momma and Daddy an elk they had killed, they knew we were starving. There were seven babies born on our homestead, but two died and our cemetery was started.

The years were full of struggle, but there was love, not only in our home, but also in many of our neighbors needed help and no one was exempt from the help of the Lawson Homestead. Momma and Daddy had aged young from all the hard work and when they could no longer handle the entire ranch demanded of them, our sister, Ida and her husband, Charles took over the running of the ranch. They are sitting behind me today along with sister Maude and our beloved sister Helen, who we all adopted along with her two sons and that is another story, but every one from, what later became the Dawson Ranch has a story. Even our neighbors came to this ranch, we all needed each other, and no one was turned away.

When the measles epidemic hit our valley Charles and Ida made room for all our neighbors to come to be doctored, no one came to vaccinate our children they said we lived too far away; I guess they didn't think our children mattered.

Charles and some of the men decided they needed to have the doctor come. So they and I won't go into the details for fear of incriminating someone here, went to town thirty miles away and brought the doctor back tied to the buggy, with all the vaccine and medicine to take care of our children.

By now, the entire room was listening and sitting forward in their chairs as Laura continued. For some it was to late, eight of our precious babies died, including one of mine and Ida's two daughters, adding more headstones in our cemetery, the neighbors buried their children there.

WW1 took its toll on our valley when it took my husband and several other young boys. Their bodies were not returned to us, we just received a letter that started, "We regret to inform you and so on." One of the very talented cowboys on the ranch made a memorial hand carved marker for them, where we could place flowers. Our little cemetery was growing, so a fence was built around it and just below the sign that read "Lawson Cemetery" was placed one that now said, "The Dawson Ranch Memorial Cemetery."

Then the Depression came, at first we weren't affected by it. We were taking care of our selves and everyone in the valley. The Dawson Ranch did not have to worry, because it was all paid for and they didn't have any debt. However, some of the other ranchers were losing theirs, they still had a mortgage. When Ida learned that some of them were having to butcher their horses to feed their families and at times only had wild turnips to eat, they built onto their bunk house and they got together with the other neighbors and they cut down trees and made lumber out of them at the sawmill. They built a two-story house that would house four families. They moved in and for the next four years we all lived off the land and we survived together as one big family. We didn't ask for any help from the government.

Maude, Helen, and some of the other women made a school for our children. The children were fed in the little house that Momma and Daddy built, in 1868.

Then WW2 came and took our boys, Helen's two sons Johnny and Joel went to war with about six other young boys. In 1943 a letter arrived from the War Department, starting; we regret to inform you your son Johnny Dandridge was killed in the line of duty, and they name some town in France that we had never heard of after him.

Another letter came shortly after, that said, your son has been awarded the Congressional Medal of Honor for his act of bravery in saving the lives of his platoon. He died fighting beyond the call of duty. He is a hero. There was much more said 'but I don't remember all that was said. Even the President of the United States sent a letter. The army wanted to bury him at the Arlington National Cemetery, but we wouldn't let them. Johnny needed to come home to Dawson City, to his family.

Laura had to stop, by now she was crying and could not talk. Ida stood and asked if she could come forward. There was sobbing all around the room, as Ida stepped into the podium. She hugged Laura then she turned and said in a soft voice, "Gentlemen, my name is Ida Ingabar Dawson, My husband Charles and I own the Dawson Ranch. What my sister Laura has told you is only part of the story of Johnny Dandridge."

We did not need a marble stone to remind us of how brave he was, and he would not have wanted a medal. Johnny was always a hero to us. He endured so much just to live. My husband Charles found him, his brother Joel and his mother living in a dirty cave where they had been abandoned. They survived by pure determination, they were the example of the will to live that was needed for the ranchers and the pioneers of our valley and I suppose of the opening of the West.

There are many stories of how we worked and endured the hardships. That war was to take the lives of six more of our sons, before it was finished. We were a city in mourning and grief for a very long time, but we knew we had to rise above it, to move on and raise the rest of the children we had. We all raised the children of our city, and we worked together comforting and helping each other through it like families do.

We have the pipe hanging over our fireplace in our modest home that our father and Chief Ouray smoked when they made the agreement to live in peace together. It is a reminder of how two nations can live in peace when they talk and keep their promises to each other. I remember the many times the Chief and some of his braves would come to our home and visit with my daddy. They became good friends. They were always welcome and they ate at our table.

Chief Ouray trusted my father enough to show him where the Indian burial grounds were located and Father would not allow any of the cattle to graze in that area. It was considered a very spiritual place. To this day no one knows of the location, in respect to the Ute Tribes that still go there." This was the first Johnny White Feather had heard this and it got all his attention as he looked at Helen with questions, She just smiled and looked away.

Now your people come to our valley and say they want to take all this from us. They say they need another reservoir and our town is the only place for it. There are 300 reservoirs and ponds on the top of the Grand Mesa. How many more do they need? We understand the farmers and growers in the valley need irrigation, but is one less reservoir going to change any thing? We told them to find another place for it, but they tell us they won't do that, because they have made up their minds they want our valley.

They will cover all the natural hot springs the Indians have used for many centuries and the meadows where the elk come in the fall to graze, there are mounds where Chief Ouray told my father were the graves of his ancestors on our ranch,

We never let the animals graze there out of respect for "The Ute Families." How can you let the BLM and the WCA cover all this up with thousands of gallons of water? Our ancestors and families are buried in the Dawson City Memorial Cemetery with so much history to tell. How can you let them just come in and say to us that we have to get out? They tell us they will relocate the graves. How can they do that when many of them are buried in a plain pine box? They would have to desecrate them and much would be lost.

I am seventy two years old and some day I want to be buried next to my momma, daddy, my children and my husband, but I want to be buried in our cemetery where our family, and ranchers are buried. We lived and will die knowing we did it all together. I was born there and I want to die there. How can you ask us to locate our bones somewhere else when we have no connection to any where else?

I don't know what else I can say to you, only that we have come to you at great expense and sacrifice. We have used all our resources to pay for this battle we have had to fight. We had over two thousand head of cattle, one thousand sheep and I don't know how many goats, but after our last roundup we have no sheep, no goats and only a hundred fifty head of cattle left, we are at the end of the road. One of our wonderful ladies sold the brass bed that was her grandmother's to help pay for this trip by train. She did it so we could come here. We are too proud to beg and we will do as you say, and we will endure, but you will be taking the heart out of the pioneers that came to make a life in the wilderness, we connected to with our sweat and blood. Please do not trample it into the ground. I said I would not beg, but please consider our plight and let us continue to live in our valley.

Then she stopped and looked at each one of the men sitting above her, and slowly turned to look at the rest of those distinguished men and women in the assembly behind her. Charles stood and walked to her, he put his arms around her and simply said, "I Love you." There were people who were trying very hard not show their emotions and hide it when they wiped the tears from their eyes.

Later, as they had all gathered in Charles and Ida's room, they all agreed they had done the best they could; now it was up to the Congress people to decide. Johnny came to Laura and Ida; he smiled and said, "Where were the two of you when our chiefs were trying to have council with the people from the Indian agencies and the delegates for Indian Affairs?"

Just then, there was a knock at the door and when Charles opened it, to his shock stood President Harry Truman, behind him were six security guards looking very stern and straight. Charles was speechless, and then the president spoke: "I am Harry Truman," he said and he smiled. Charles finally was able to speak. "Yes, Mr. President I know who you are, it is my great honor to see you, and I apologize for my rudeness, please come in." He stepped back and the president entered the room, as he entered the guards lined the hall and stood at attention.

After the introductions the president held Laura's hand and told her, he listened to her oration in the Halls of Congress and she was very good, and has she ever considered writing his speeches. She smiled, blushed and said, "Thank you, but I already have a job."

He laughed, and then he turned to Ida and said, that he was very proud to meet her. He and Bess would like it very much if all of your delegation of ranchers would honor them with a luncheon at the White House tomorrow. He had something he would like to discuss with them that they might find interesting. She said, "They would like that very much."

"Good, then I will have a car here about 10:30 to pick them up, by the way how many of you are there?" Then he was gone. They all looked at each other, and then they looked at Johnny and asked, "What could he possibly mean?" Johnny said, "I have no idea."

Next morning everyone was waiting under the canopy at the front doors, when three big black shiny Cadillac's pulled up in front of the hotel. From each car, two men in black suits stepped out and opened the door to the car escorting the Dawson group to their seats inside. It was such a luxurious car, the likes, as they had never seen before. Charles pressed one of the buttons, much to Ida's dismay, telling him, "Don't touch anything, they might make you pay for it or worse take you to jail if you break it."

He told her, "Don't be silly, why would they put anything in one of these cars if it would break so easily." So he pushed the button, a drawer opened, and there were small bottles of some kind of liquid in them. Then he read the label and it said vodka, the next one said Jack Daniels. He laughed and said, "Anyone want a drink before we see the president?" Everyone declined, laughing.

They entered through a tunnel leading to a garage, and the President and Mrs. Truman were there to greet them as they exited the cars. They shook hands with everyone as the

President introduced Bess to them, as if they did not know her. Then they were taken to a very nice private room where a table was set with the finest china, but first Mr. Truman asked if anyone would like a glass of wine, everyone declined, and of course, Charles had to tell him about the nice liquor cabinet in the car. The President just smiled and raised his eyebrows. "Yes, I have heard about those. They don't put one in the car I ride in though." Bess was the nicest woman Ida had ever met, she knew all about the old home cooking and she even told about how she would help her mother can vegetables in the fall.

Everyone felt so at home with them, it did not seem like they were talking to the President of the United States and the First Lady. The luncheon was just delicious but was over too soon. President Truman did have other duties, so he suggested they all come with him to the Oval Office. Mrs. Truman said her good-byes and left the room.

In the Oval Office, he became very serious, when he said, "I have been listening while you were talking to the Congress and I believe I have come up with a solution you might like, to help you solve your predicament. I am sure Mr. White Feather has heard of the Antiquity Act that President Theodore Roosevelt enacted in 1906. It has to do with preserving the historical and geological sites from being destroyed by looters and people who have no regard for the environment.

"I believe you fall into this category, but you will have to follow certain guidelines. Your attorney and I will go over the details and he will explain all of the rules to you then you can discuss it and decide what you want, and if we agree then we will have a contract made up and we will all sign it. After which time I will present it to Congress and if they agree, although I do not really need their approval, I will sign it into law. I want to make sure it can never be changed, once I sign it."

Johnny stayed with the President while everyone else shook hands and said their good-byes and then went back to the hotel.

They tried to be cheerful, but their hearts were not into it, they were so scared. For the rest of the afternoon everyone just walked around making small talk, then they went to the dining room where so many people that had heard of their speech in Congress and tried to encourage them greeted them, but they just could not be cheerful. They knew their entire lives and the lives of the entire Dawson City community depended on them.

It was late when Johnny finally came back to the hotel. He had a briefcase full of papers, he was very serious when he walked into the room, then very slowly he smiled, and said, "I think this is doable."

Under the 1950 Sub Chapter LX1 National and International Monument and Memorial, Section 431 Act September 20, 1950, the land acreage was increased to the maximum 100 acres to be placed under the control of the Government of the United States, to be decreed as a National Historical sites and Memorials, and shall be confined to the smallest area compatible with the proper care and management of the objects to be protected.

When objects situated on tract of land covered by an bona fide imperfect claim or held in private ownership, the tract or so much there of is not properly kept in care of the object, shall then be relinquished to the management of the United

States Government and the Secretary of the Interior shall authorize to except the relinquishment of the tract in behalf of the U.S. Government.

In 1935 the revision of the Antiquities Act for Historical sites Section 2 article 2, stated that the must be a survey taken of the claimed historical and archeological site to certify it as to determine the exceptional value as commemorating or illustrating the history of the United States.

Section F: Restore, reconstruct and rehabilitate preserve and maintain historical and prehistoric sites, buildings, objects and preserve the properties of national historical or archaeological significance.

Section H: Operating and managing historical sites, buildings and properties acquired under provision of this act to benefit the public and to charge a fee for visitation and grant concession leases or permits to use the land building space shall be let to competition bidding to the person making the highest best bid.

After Johnny finished reading the provisions to everyone, they all started asking questions at once. What did competitive bidding mean? Do we have to make a bid every year just to keep our property? What would happen if some big corporation decided to come and out bid us, we wouldn't be able to out bid them? We are not rich.

Johnny said that would be a concern for us to bring before the president. There was one more thing Ida said, "The Indian Burial Grounds are located outside of the 100 acre boundary of our ranch. It is located about 175 acres from the north of the ranch, but it would be in the direct path of the proposed Reservoir." Ida said her father took her there, so she would know in the event he should die and know one would know its location.

Johnny said, "That would be something I believe the Ute Indian Nation would have to be a part of preserving, and I happen to know a man who is the Nephew of Chief Ouray, he was about ten years old when your father and Ouray made their agreement. He was there. He is very old, but he is very much with his own mind and I will contact him to make sure of his recollections."

We will have to have proof of all our claims, and there will be Government people who will come to Dawson City to inspect the significance of it being a Historical City, then we will have to submit our own desires. I have talked to the president and I do believe he wants to save our city.

Everyone was anxious about all this and did not want to rush into a decision that would be wrong, but they also did not want to give up their rights of the City to the government. Johnny said we will sleep on all this then tomorrow when we have all had a good rest we will go piece by piece over every word of this contract, and make a decision, as for me I am very tired and could use a bite to eat, a shower and sleep. Everyone agreed, then Charles stepped over to him and said, "Johnny we appreciate everything you are doing for us, we could not have done any of this by our selves." Everyone in the room nodded and said thank you.

Helen had not said anything up until now, but she finally said, "I have prayed to the Great Spirit many times to find my family of the Ute Tribe, and he sent me you, my brother, I shall forever be grateful." Johnny said, "I too have prayed for you."

The next day they called for room service, because no one

wanted to be disturbed while they went over all the provisions of the contract line by line. At noon they sent for room service again and by that evening they had finished.

First and most importantly, they did not want to relinquish their ranches or the city to the complete control of the government, they still wanted to have the final say as to what it was to be used for, after all there were still working ranches there. They did not want to have their homes and ranches put up for bids. They agreed all buildings and archeological sites would be maintained and properly cared for as long as one or more or the original family of Lawsons and Dawsons remained there, at which time it would then be relinquished to the care of the United States

Government. Financial compensation from the Department of the Interior during times of need would be accepted with the provision that all debts would be paid back.

There shall be proof of the agreement from Chief Ouray's nephew, Jack Running with Bear. There shall also be proof of the Indian Mounds, but only two persons from the government shall be present, as not to disturb the ancestors, and it shall be kept a secret as to the exact location, to prevent anyone else from going there. Also the provision of 100 acres shall be extended to 175 acres, to include the burial grounds as to the Historical and Archaeological sites there in.

The out buildings shall remain as they originally were constructed, with the exception of provisions for electricity, water and sewer, which shall be provided for with the aid of the Department of Interior.

No other building or residents shall be added to the 175

acres at any time there after, without the approval of the Department of the Interior or the United States Government.

The Dawson City Memorial Cemetery shall remain as it is, with the exception that it shall be revised beneath to say:

Dawson City Memorial Cemetery
In Memory of
John and Ingabar Lawson
Established 1868

There were a few minor things they wanted, but in all they were satisfied, telling Johnny to submit it to President, Harry S. Truman, and hopefully he would be able to give them an answer soon, so they could go back and tell everyone the good news. Ida especially wanted to tell the BLM and the WCA where they could stick their reservoir, personally.

It was another four days before they received an answer, but when Johnny came back, they were all sitting in the dining room. He came in with the papers in his hand waving them over his head, you could hear him shouting above everyone in the dining room, "We won, we won." He was no longer the sophisticated lawyer, he did a little Indian dance around the tables to get to their table, and then he took Laura's arm and gave her a big hug. Telling her she did it, with her speech in the Halls of Congress.

They voted for everything we presented to them. The President was elated and he signed it into an Act. Dawson City cannot be touched or change hands for as long as there is still one Lawson or Dawson living on the land. There is to be a home for the aged to live in next to the cemetery and it will be dedicated to the Lawson Family. There is so much more for me to tell you, but now all you have to do is sign on the dotted line in front of witnesses and Dawson City is yours for all time.

Ida could not contain herself any longer as she broke into tears, everyone in the restaurant was cheering, and even the very high-class clientele raised their wine glasses and gave a salute. There were hugs and smiles. "Oh yes there is one more thing I have to tell you, first President and Mrs. Truman wish to come to Dawson City to visit next spring, and also all expenses for this trip coming here and returning is paid for by your government. You will not be taking a train but flying First Class on the official airplane of the United States of America, then driven home in a limousine, and the president said with a smile I might add, with a liquor bar if you want one," they all laughed. Now all they wanted was to go home, and celebrate with all their friends and families.

When they got home and all the neighbors were gathered in the front yard to greet them, they were in awe of the big black limousines and the very impressive men that got out with the returning "victors". Many hugs all around and everyone talking at the same time, They even gave the limo drivers a big hug, which they felt a bit uncomfortable with, but after it was explained, " that's how we do it here," they just joined in. There was a huge community party where Johnny got up on the back of a wagon and explained it all to everyone. It was agreed, they could do everything that was written there. They all had to see the signature of the President. It was a very festive week.

For the next two months there were Government officials coming and going. Johnny was able to get Jack Runs with Bears come and show where the Indian burial mounds were and he told where the meeting with Chief Ouray and John Lawson was and where they smoked the pipe to seal their agreement. Lots of pictures were taken of the site, but it was sealed off by the Ute Indian council after they had inspected it also. They had a special ceremony for the ancestors and prayed to the Great Spirit to protect it, so no one could get to it and a special one to rid the site of all the intruders who had violated the site by being there.

There was a large home built for the elderly people of the valley to stay who were unable to care for them selves, beside the cemetery, with the original lilacs from Ingabar's yard and her beautiful blue spruce were trimmed and refurbished to live another hundred years. Everything was made into a wonderful garden with lots of flowers.

As for the reservoir, it was started down valley, about ten miles from Dawson City. It soon dried up, amounting to nothing. Eventually the grass grew back and some aspen trees sprouted again, but it was used mostly for grazing. The one thing Ida wanted to do most of all was to sent a copy of the contract to the B.L.M. and the W.C.A. with the hand written message on the bottom of the page that said,. "Don't ever try to bully the town of Dawson City, again. She sent a copy of the contract to the BLM and the WCA. In addition, at the bottom of the page she wrote, "Don't ever try to bully the town of Dawson City again. There is no length we will not go to fight to keep our land. Then she signed it Ida Ingabar (Lawson) Dawson.

Two years later, we lost our beloved Laura. She was buried next to her husband and her little daughter. There was a large group of people who came all the way from the Ute

Indian Nation in Utah and even a couple of representatives from Denver came. Grand Junction furnished a bus to bring the older people who could not drive the distance to come and pay their respects to a very courageous "lady." Ida, Maude, Helen, Charles and Laura's remaining daughter, Dottie, stood together holding hands, surrounded by all their friends and neighbors. It was a sad day for all who knew her.

The town of Dawson City worked hard to restore many of the buildings that had started to crumble from age. There was a bank building built. In addition, a new grocery store, the hardware store refurbished from the old grocery store. The last thing was a gas station, but the one thing not everyone wanted was the saloon, but it got out voted and was built out of logs and chinked to look like one of the old building, so it was allowed, but with restrictions. No dance hall girls, it was used for town meetings whenever the occasion arose. The only thing that wasn't there was a church, but that wouldn't have been part of the original town, so one was build outside of the town boundary.

At first there were many tourists, but eventually most people wanted to go to a place with more excitement and would go to the bigger cities, when it was made very clear motorcycles and off road buggies were not welcomed. They soon found other places to go, during those years there were the hippies and the flower child group that would try to settle in town. However, when they found they were sprayed with paint to many times they even got discouraged, then about the 1960's things started to quiet down, much to everyone's delight. With the Vietnam War starting there were more important things to think about.

The ranches started to thrive and the cattle grazed the open range but they were separated from the sheep, and they were alternated each year. Everyone settled into a happy existence. Charles had turned almost all of the ranching over to Charlie and his young grandson Charles the third or as everyone called him Chuck. He was young to be running a ranch, but he had become quite a cowboy and he seemed to have a good sense of the finances. He would help Ida with the books and keeping the records.

The winter of 1965 started early, the summer had been very hot and dry, the river had almost dried up, it was difficult to get water for the cattle, but by middle July the monsoons started and it rained every day. So far they had only had one hay crop, so the ranchers had to pool all their resources and buy hay to stock up for the winter, this was not cheap and a few of the ranchers just took a lot of their cattle to market early. Not getting full price for them at the stock yards, but it was still cheaper then trying to feed them for the winter.

Charlie had talked it over with Charles and Chuck, they decided to take some of the older cattle down, but if they kept half of the already bred cows they would have a new batch of calves in the spring and maybe they wouldn't be hurt too much.

The monsoons lasted into the latter part of August and the sun came out just giving the ranchers enough time to drive a herd down to Grand Junction and the train yards. It was a difficult drive, one of the ranchers wives drove the chuck wagon, but could not cross the Dawson Creek and had to turn back. It had over flowed its banks. At first, they were going to divert the route to Delta, but decided to try to get all the cattle across at one of the more shallow spots, but it turned out to be muddy and some of the cattle would sink in it and have to be dragged out by the cowboys. They lost thirteen steers that way, but eventually got across.

One of the young cowboys, the son of the James Ranch drowned that same day. He was tangled in the rope as he tried to get one of the steers out of the mud. Before anyone could get to him, he and his horse fell into the current. Between the horse fighting to get his footing and the panicked steer, he didn't have a chance of being saved. They found his body about a mile down stream tangled in the rope and the dead steer, somehow the horse had managed to get out, but he was standing on the opposite bank. A somber group arrived at the stockyards three days later. They had wrapped young Billy James in blankets and draped him over the back of his horse leading him to town. They brought him home to be buried in the Dawson Cemetery.

Winter came with a vengeance. It started October 3 with a blizzard that lasted for three days. There was snow piled high on the west sides of all the buildings, closing the main street. There were people staying in the schoolhouse and the motel. Dottie tried to feed everyone, but was running out of food. Finally, after the storm subsided, and the town began to rally, they had a meeting in the saloon and decided to put up a stock of food in the old root cellar, which was still being used for the cheese. There was enough room for some smoked and dried meat, so everyone got busy and was donating to get it filled.

The winter was just beginning, and no one could be sure of how the rest would be. This town knew how to survive and they always planned preparing for the worst. The rest of the cattle were brought down from the high country, a mountain lion had already gotten a few of the sheep, before they could round them up. There was a big lion hunt organized within the week. They not only got the lion, but they also bagged six Elk and five deer to cook up and can. All the men and women got together for a Community canning day. There were smoke ovens set up to prepare the meat and a hog was butchered where all the hams were smoked. All the fat from the pig was melted down and placed in glass containers for rendered lard. Everything was stored in the cellar. Some of the ranchers took some food home with them to store in their own cellars. No matter how much they planned, ahead they could not have anticipated how this winter was going to change many things. They felt they were about as prepared as they could get.

Then the snow started to fall again. Every night there would be two feet of snow for weeks on end. Some of the boys from the school would get up on the roofs and shovel snow off. The load was getting heavy and everyone in town was afraid they would collapse. They had a snow plow, but eventually there was no place to put all the snow.

The Clark Benson's house caught on fire. They had five children who were asleep at the time in the upstairs bedrooms. The small fire truck that no one thought would ever have to use could not get out of the fire station. No one had thought to plow the parking lot that day and there was two feet of snow up against the bay doors. All five of the children were killed and Clark made Ella Mae run for help but when he went back inside, trying to rescue the children, he was overcome by the smoke and died as well.

The whole town was in a state of disbelief and grief. They had a meeting where one of the firefighters volunteered to take Ella Mae in until she could be taken down to Grand Junction to be with her folks, as soon as they could get the sleigh through the snow. She wasn't able to function in any way on her own, and she just gave up on living, and lost her mind.

It was a constant struggle to keep all the cattle from being buried in the snow and keeping them fed. They were running out of hay to feed them. By April everyone was exhausted and at their wits end. Dottie's restaurant and motel was housing so many of the families who just couldn't maintain their own houses. Some of the roofs had caved in and left them with nothing. They were able to save a few clothes and belongings, but there were so many of people.

When the snow started to melt in the high country they had another obstacle to face, the water in the river had risen to flood stage, and sand bags had to be made and placed along the riverbank. Mainly to save the old homestead house and Maude's cabin. Everyone helped set up sand bags and were able to save the cabin.

This time the Federal Government stepped in and supplied the town with sandbags, food and people to help fight the floodwaters. Then the construction of the damaged roofs began. They were supported by placing logs under the original roofs to add support in the future if this happened again. In addition, the Grand Junction Fire District donated two new fire trucks and a red brick fire station was built next to the schoolhouse. A huge snowplow was donated to the City of Dawson. In addition, a maintenance yard, just outside the limits of the city boundary was built, across from the

Church. One of the men who lived in Dawson City was hired by Mesa. It would be his job to keep a road open at all times, winter and summer.

The town voted to build a levy to keep any water in the spring from flowing towards Dawson City to protect the old Homestead and any other buildings along the river. A bridge was built across the river, where the sawmill was located.

There were no more winters like that one again, but in the fall, everyone prepared for it anyway. The fall of 1968, Helen Dandridge became gravely ill, she didn't know what the matter was, but she refused to go to the doctor in Grand Junction. She took her own home remedies, but nothing seemed to help and she died in December. Maude took it very hard, they had been lifetime friends and Maude just never was able to rally from the loss. She died that next summer.

Charles was ninety-four by now and Ida was eighty-nine. She could no longer take care of her beloved Charles, so the family decided he should go to the Dawson City home for the aged. He was not happy with that arrangement, but realized Ida could not care for him, as she would have insisted on doing. She said, "I have taken care of this man for sixty nine years and I can't think of anyone else doing my job." She fought it harder than he did. She just could not imagine him not sleeping next to her at night, but in the end, she had to let him go there, but she would walk there every day to have her meals with him, then Charlie would take her home and wait until she went to bed and was asleep before he left.

There was always someone staying with her all night in case she woke in the middle of the night, she had a tendency to get up and start to walk to the home to see if Charles was okay. In the spring of 1971, she was sitting with him, when he looked at her and said, “My dear wife, it is time for me to leave you, and I want to know you will be alright until we are together again. I have loved you with all my heart and I am so glad I found you that day out there in the pasture. You were so beautiful, I will always see you that way. We have lived a great life, had our children and built our ranch together. We have more memories than most people would ever dream of having. My love, I will wait for you when you come to me again with my arms open. I love you,” and he slipped away. She held his hand to her lips and whispered, “I love you, my beloved,” and kissed them for the last time.

His funeral was the biggest one Dawson City had ever seen. People crowded into the cemetery and many who couldn’t get close stood outside the fence in the parking lot. President Nixon sent a special blue spruce tree to be planted in his honor. Sending his condolences and saying this was a true American pioneer who helped to build the west. The American flag was flown at half mast in the capital in Denver in his honor, and a moment of silence was help in Grand Junction.

Ida just couldn’t stay in their home much longer, she wouldn’t eat and she would wander around that big house and touch things that were Charles’ and talk to him as if he were there. Dottie would bring her meals and sit with her making sure she ate all of it. Ida had so many friends coming and going all the time. Everyone worried about her and for the next two years she live in the house with her memories.

Charlie was getting up there in years also and he could not care for her the way he wanted. Chuck had gone off to college and he was dating a girl he finally married, bringing her back to Dawson, hoping she would love it as much as he did, but that was not to be. She just was not cut out to be a rancher's wife. Chuck had his own ranch by now and was the owner of the Dawson City Bank. His new wife left and went back to the big city of Chicago, and filed for a divorce.

His father, Charlie was ailing with a cough he just could not seem to get rid of. He was finally diagnosed with a respiratory disease that was not going to get any better, so he was placed in a hospital in Grand Junction and he died a month later. After that, the decisions were up to Chuck, Dottie and Lorrie, so they had a council and decided it was time for Grandma Ida to be taken out of her home and arrangements were made to make her a home at the same place where Charles had been living. In the Dawson City Nursing Home, the name had been changed to Pleasant Valley Nursing Home.

Oh, what a fight that was, as she was so angry and would not talk to any of them for a long time. Finally, there were people coming and going all the time to see her and she finally decided she was not as miserable as she thought she was going to be. She rallied and was happy with her new home. For the next years she made sure, she was the feistiest little old woman there and she was quite the fun woman of the home. She made friends and always had a happy thing to say to everyone, the only thing she could not tolerate were the reporters that were always trying to get her to tell them the secret to long life. She would tell them, she would have a couple of shots of whiskey before bedtime and she made it a practice of minding her own business. They weren't sure if she was telling the truth or not, because she would laugh her head off when they finally gave up and left.

Lorrie would look at her and shake her finger at her and say, "Now Grandma, why would you tell him that?"

Grandma Ida would just grin and say, "Ah, shucks, was I bad?" Then she would laugh.

100 YEARS, LOOKING BACK

As Shannon sat with Grandma she could see, she was tiring. Maybe, she thought it was time for a reprieve for a little while, so she stayed in her cabin and did a little catch up on her writing. She also hadn't been in touch with her boss for a while. She wasn't sure if she wanted to share the entire story of The Dawson family. She was taught when she went to Journalism School not to get too involved with your story, to stay professional, but Shannon had become involved. Grandma Ida was not just a story subject to her anymore. She was the grandmother she never had, and the family she had lost in a car accident. An aunt, who had loved her, raised her and Shannon loved her aunt, but she was gone now also, so she didn't have a family anymore.

Lorrie had become the sister she never had and Charles had become very important in her life. She knew it would be the hardest thing for her to leave them. Charles had started to come over in the morning and sit with her out near the river for his morning coffee, and she looked so forward to him. He never said how he felt about her, but each time he left, he would kiss her on the cheek, as he did Grandma. She wanted more from him, but was afraid to say anything, he would think she was silly, she feared.

One morning she mentioned to him, what he thought about taking Grandma for a short walk around town. She thought many of the townsfolk would very much love to see her. He thought it was a good idea, if Grandma would agree and was able, she is spry, but she tires very quickly. They went together to ask Grandma if she would like that, and to their surprise she said she would like that very much, as long as they both came along. They agreed and next day when they came to get her at the home, she was dressed in her nicest powder blue dress. One of the nurses had come in, and combed and fixed her hair. She looked lovely and so sweet, but she insisted on wearing the old hat, she had always worn when they were a working ranch, saying, no one would recognize her with out it. Shannon had to smile at that. Lorrie came also just in case she was needed; she had a wheel chair that she followed behind with as they walked in, the event Grandma would like to rest occasionally.

Grandma was excited to see all the stores and all the people; she laughed and visited with everyone. All the store-keepers would come and talk. Some of the old timers would reminisce with her about the old times. Grandma had balked when Lorrie brought the wheel chair, but she was grateful for it when she needed to stop and rest.

When Charles suggested they go to Dottie's for lunch, Grandma was especially anxious. Shannon was to learn that the restaurant was the home John and Ingabar had originally built, but Charles had restored many of the things, adding a bathroom and electricity so many years ago, refurbishing the old bunk house, into the motel it is today.

Charles had called ahead to let Dottie know Grandma was

coming, and she had fixed the restaurant up special for the occasion. She had put out some of the old furnishings that were there when Charles and Ida lived there. She hung the peace pipe on the mantle that Great Grandpa John had shared with Chief Ouray. The linens on the table were the ones Ida had used. Today, Dottie had very carefully washed each plate and utensil with love that were Ida's and Charles setting them on the table with all the silverware she had stored. She polished all of them just for this occasion. Many of the people who had been in the valley for so many years had come just to see Ida. There were pictures hung showing the old ranch and the deer hunts with Maude. Helen wore a wide grin, as she looked at the children from the school. The best thing Dottie had kept, no one knew about was the old wide brimmed hat that Charles always wore, is was so stained from many years of sweat, but it still held it's shape and Dottie had left it just as it was.

Grandma slowly walked up the steps to the porch; many of the neighbors she knew stood and welcomed her reaching out to touch her hand. They were afraid to touch her, she was so tiny and they thought they might break her, but she would reach out and with a firm grip took their hand and spoke to each of them. As she entered the door, everyone just stood and clapped their hands. She seemed embarrassed by all the attention. Every one watched her, as she looked around at all the things. Ida took her time as she walked around the room, remembering, touching some of the pictures and when she saw Charles hat she almost started to cry. Charles took her arm and steadying her, and then she walked to all the people and smiled. She looked at Jackson who must have been close to ninety-five himself and had been with them when they and shook hands with the President. She smiled and poked him in the stomach, telling him that she thought he was dead. He just laughed and said, "He couldn't die just yet, he wanted to wait for her to see what else she had in store for everyone."

Then she went to another old timer and asked him, something. He said, "I remember you used to be a pretty good dancer once, do you still dance?" She just laughed and said, "Not for quite a while."

Another of the old timers asked her if she remembered the "Sheep Herding Rodeo, when the cowboys thought it would be no problem herding a "bunch" of sheep? She had to laugh about that and said, "Oh yes, I do remember that, and I also remember you were the one who suggested they do it."

Finally, Dottie showed them to their table, and when Ida saw all the linens and how nice it looked with all her old dishes and silver, she looked at Dottie and smiled. "I didn't think any of those old dishes were still around," she said.

"Grandma, I have all of them, I remember eating at your table and thinking they were so pretty with all those flowers painted on them. I will cherish them forever." Grandma said, "They are just old dishes, you need some new ones." She couldn't hide how glad she was to see them again.

"Oh, I have some that I use for every day," Dottie said, "but they don't make them like these any more." As everyone sat down and they had finished eating their lunch, Grandma looked at Charles and then she looked at Shannon, and then a smile came over her face as she remembered something her daddy had said, one time after he had looked at Charles and her. "So." Ida looked at Charles and said, "Charles do you like Shannon?" He was startled by that question. He looked at

Shannon and she looked at him, he replied. "Well, yes I do."

Grandma said, "You know I'm not getting any younger, so when are you going to pop the question?" Charles remembered how this turned out for his grandpa and Grandma Ida, so he decided to play along with her and replied, "Now what question would that be, Grandma?"

She liked this game and said, "You know darn well what question."

Charles got out of his chair and walked around the table turned Shannon's chair facing him, got down on one knee and said, "Shannon I don't know for sure how to ask this, it seems a little to soon, but I love you and I can't imagine my live would amount to a hill of beans if you were not in it. I can only hope you feel the same as I do, I love you and would you consider being my wife?"

Shannon was so surprised, she was crying. "Oh Charles, I knew from the first time I saw you I loved you, yes, yes, yes I will be your wife and I will love you for the rest of my life." Ida laughed and said, "Well, okay then, Dottie, what's for dessert?" Everyone let out a cheer and everyone was laughing as Charles kissed Shannon for the first time on the lips.

They were married in the garden behind Maude's house next to the river where Ida and Charles had exchanges their vows seventy-one years ago. Shannon had asked Ida if she would give her away and Lorrie was her maid of honor. Charles had Joel stand up with him as the honored man and Lorrie's husband was his best man, they left for a two-week honeymoon in the Virgin Islands.

When they returned Shannon called her boss and told him she quit her job as a journalist that she had decided to be a cowgirl instead. He was pretty mad, but she really didn't care. She told him the story of Ida wasn't designed for just an article in the newspaper that she was going to make it a Novel instead, there was far too much to tell.

For the next weeks she would go out to the valley with Charles, spending time riding his beautiful quarter horses and seeing what this ranch was all about, and it didn't take long for her to fall in love with every tree, blade of grass and river that flowed through it. She blended into this way of life as if she was born to it.

She continued to talk to Grandma Ida and one day Ida said, "Shannon would you walk with me to the cemetery?"

Shannon said, "Of course," and took her arm as they slowly walked among the flowers, the lilacs and the tall blue spruce that was just a sprig when Daddy planted it. Grandma would explain these things as they walked.

Ida looked around and said, "You know there have been so many changes, and many of them for the good. I like little bench that someone made in the center of the cemetery, so we can come and just sit and remember. There are so many more markers and headstones now. As she pointed to them one at a time she would say their names. There is Virginia, my little sister, and Ellie, the very first grave, and Clemens and his son. He committed suicide because he couldn't face the death of his only son who was killed in the war, Aully, Helen, Maude, Momma and Daddy, and all the children who died from the measles epidemic.

"I can tell you something about every one here. Do you realize that in every cemetery in the world every grave has a story to tell, everyone has a history. I have out lived just about everyone that started here in this valley.

"I am going to tell you something that my Charles told me, after Helen had died. One day I found him sitting outside looking at the valley and there was a look on his face of great sadness, he had been crying, now mind you He didn't cry too often, so I just sat next to him and let him talk.

"He said, 'Do you remember when I came home with Johnny and Joel after trapper Dandridge had almost killed Helen and Maude?' As I nodded, He continued, 'I had traveled all over the Mesa looking for them. I finally found them about where I had found Helen and the boys living in that cave. Joel was sitting kneeled down and Johnny was next to his, they had painted their faces with the black ashes from the fire pit, and then they had smeared them selves with blood. Johnny was naked to his underwear and Joel was the same. It took me a while to figure out where all the blood had come from. Then I saw, hanging like a deer when you skin it to gut and butcher was Trapper Dandridge. His legs were tied spread eagle naked between two trees; He had been skinned and gutted. I was pretty sure he wasn't dead when it was done. 'Oh My God,' was all I could say.

He said, "As I started to approach them, Joel raised his hand palm out, indicating for me to stop as He slightly turned to look at me, with the most threatening look on his face. Johnny never looked at me, he was in another world, there was no sign of human about him, and He was like an animal, a predator. He would have killed me I'm sure if I would have stepped between him and his prey, the trapper Dandridge. I stepped back and just watched, there was nothing I could do.

"Johnny finally stood, he had a large knife in his hand, that he had been sharpening all the while he was squatting next to the fire, I hadn't noticed it before. He slowly walked to the carcass, proceeded to dismember it one arm at a time then the head and so on until all that was left were the two legs hanging there." I told Charles to stop, "I didn't want to hear any more." But he couldn't, he just continued talking, not hearing my plea. He said, "I have to tell it to someone, I have kept this inside of me all these years, Ida, I am so sorry it had to be you, I know how much you loved those boys, but they weren't our boys any more, they were something else, they weren't even human. Joel didn't participate in this ritual, He only watched. Johnny cut the rest of the body down, and then he dragged all the body parts off and threw them into the woods for the animals to devour. It was then that he noticed me standing there. It was like he woke up; he looked down at his hands and his body, he was in shock. He kept shaking his head, and looking at his hands."

"I hated him," He was crying by now. "I hated him for what he did to my mother. I hated him for what he did to her, Joel and me. How he violated her while we watched and then he would laugh and say this how you handle a savage woman. He would get drunk and beat us. Oh, God, how I hated him. There was always the fear he would come for us. Now, he will never touch or hurt us again. I have to wash him off me."

He then looked around and seeing the river, he turned and walked in until his head was under the water. Joel stood and said, "I tried to stop him when he found the trapper, with his traps, but Johnny was obsessed I couldn't stop him. He attacked like a wild animal, He was in the Dark Spirit World; and Trapper didn't know where he came from and didn't have time to fight back or to reach his knife or gun. Johnny knocked him unconscious and tied him up like a deer, then he sat down and painted his face, and body and then he undressed me and painted mine. Then we waiting for Trapper to wake up."

"Johnny spoke in a voice I didn't recognize, Do you remember us? We are your sons, but as of today I will cut your blood from us and let it flow to the dirt where it belongs. Your body will be left for the animals to eat like you left us for the animals to eat." Trapper tried to plead for his life, but Johnny was deaf and heard nothing but the voice of his hate. He skinned Trapper Dandridge; his screams could be heard for a long distance, and then Johnny slowly cut him from brisket to his manly parts, all the time Trapper screamed, until he just stopped. We sat at the fire for many hours, until you found us."

Joel stopped talking and then he said, "He is my brother again now all his hate has been used and is gone. Now we wash away the blood and all the revenge we have held inside is gone." Then he turned and walked to the water and dove in.

Ida sat next to Shannon in silence for a short time. She said, "My Charles must have died a million deaths for many years remembering that entire horrible scene, but he never judged the boys, maybe deep down inside he felt the same way. He wanted to kill that trapper when he found them in that dirty cave. He said, "I'm not sure how I felt, but at the time I wanted to see this man suffer, and perhaps I was enjoying this, not able to stop it if I could have." I think he understood how they felt.

"It is good he never told this while Helen was alive, she would never have believed this kind of hate could come out of these boys. It doesn't change a thing though, Johnny was a hero to us all, and we loved him so much. He was always so gentle and kind to everyone after that and he loved his mother with his every being. He cared for her and never left her side. Helen died in 1960 from pneumonia no one knew how old she was; no one knew when she was born only that she was the daughter of a Ute Chief.

"Laura died two years after she gave that powerful speech in the hall of Congress in Washington, D.C. She never really got to see the results of the grant given to Dawson City, through the Antiquities Act. If it wasn't for her I don't think we would be sitting here in this lovely garden and cemetery talking.

"My Charles died in 1971. He was ninety six years old. Everyone in the valley and people came from all over the country for his funeral. It would have embarrassed him, he wasn't much for all the fanfare where he was concerned, he just figured he live the best way he knew how, to love with all his heart, to give all he could even if it meant he went without. To work one hundred percent side by side with your neighbor to help each other, and when he told me that day so long ago, when he asked me to marry him that he would love me until the day he died, he did just that. He loved me with all his heart and every day he would tell me that. I never went to bed without those being the last word he whispered to me. We were married for seventy-one wonderful years, and I can hardly wait till I join him again.

There was a huge celebration for Grandma Ida on her 100th birthday and there were people Ida didn't even know there. She received a letter from the President and Mrs. Carter, wishing her happy birthday. They sent a beautiful blue spruce to join the one sent by President Nixon when Charles died.

By now, with Grandma Ida's blessing Shannon published her book, and titled it simply *Grandma Ida*. After a year a young man about thirty five years old came to the nursing home where Ida was. He walked to her and very gently gave her a hug. He said his name was Jackson Cord the third.

He continued to tell her his great grandfather was the Jack Cord, the wagon master that brought the wagon train with Johnny and Ingabar to Colorado. He was the one who helped them build their barn and the old house in 1866. He told her how Grandpa Jack would talk about Johnny and Ingabar all the time. He had wanted to come back, but he couldn't. He had gone to Alaska where he did strike it rich and he married and had two more sons. One of the boys that had gone with him was killed in a gun fight over a gold claim. Jackson, my father lived until he was sixty then he died of syphilis, please don't ask me about that. I didn't know about Dawson City until I accidentally picked up a book and started reading about the Lawson Ranch in Colorado, I couldn't put the book down.

"I knew it had to be 'the' Johnny Lawson. I had to come to see for myself. I am so honored to finally meet the daughter of the man my grandpa never stopped talking about, I felt like I already knew you. I would be so proud if you would sign this book for me."

Ida said she doesn't write so well anymore, but she would be happy to sign it, that Shannon was the one who wrote it and you should have her sign it for you. He said he would do that. They sat and talked for a long time, he told her about Jack Cord's life after he left this beautiful valley, and then he said he had to leave, but he would like to come back. Grandma Ida just laughed and said, "You had better hurry, because I'm getting pretty old." They laughed and he said, "You are the feisty one aren't you?"

EPILOGUE

Grandma Ida got to see her great great grandson before she died; He was named Charles Samuel Dawson the 4th. She died at 105 in her sleep peacefully and was laid to rest beside her beloved Charles. The inscription read, "Together we lived and loved and together we will love and walk together for eternity".

Shannon was sitting on the bench in the cemetery that morning with her arm around her son. She was telling him about all the headstones in the cemetery. "Did you know that every headstone has a history and a story to tell? There is Aunt Maude, now she was a real rancher's daughter; she could shoot like no one else, over there is your great grandma Ida. A real pioneer woman."

Shannon wanted her son to know the history and where he came from and all the people that made up the family he was honored to be a part of.

THE END

CPSIA information can be obtained
at www.ICGtesting.com
Printed in the USA
FSOW01n1406240116
16099FS